YO-BPT-225

GONIA

R. KHORDA   BISILTAN

KHORDAIM ISLES

BAVARI HILLS

BAY of SHARKS

BAVARI

THE GREAT MASOURN TRAIL

CARCOS RANGE

OULD

HERDOS

HIKAS

GOLOGO

DESSI

CHASM of GORGORON

R. VOI

DALOBU

SERPENT SWAMP

ELZIAN

COLOCANA

HEAVEN'S CHAIR MT.

LON

LIO

BAY of LON

INS   MOUNTAINS   JUNGLE

ERTS   SWAMP

LS   OASIS   DISTANCE IN MILES

0   25   50   75   100

N

The bearer of this scroll, namely,

Daniel

is a master in the
Order of the Kai

You are the warrior, Lone Wolf, last of the Kai Masters of Sommerlund and sole survivor of the massacre that destroyed your kinsmen during a bitter war with your age-old enemies, the Darklords of Helgedad. You have given your solemn pledge to restore the Kai to their former glory, ensuring the security of your land in the years to come.

Diligent study of the tome called *The Book of the Magnakai* has enabled you to master only three of the ten Magnakai Disciplines. Now, you must fulfill your pledge by completing the quest first undertaken by *Sun Eagle* over one thousand years ago.

It is a quest that will take you deep into Castle Death — a dangerous journey not completed successfully since the time of the *Sun Eagle*.

Joe Dever, co-author of the Lone Wolf series, is a contributing editor to *White Dwarf,* Britain's leading role-playing games magazine, and editor of the 'World of Lone Wolf' series. Lone Wolf is the culmination of seven years of developing the world of Magnamund. He is the author of *The Magnamund Companion* and *The Legends of Lone Wolf* novels.

Gary Chalk, co-author and illustrator of the *Lone Wolf* series, was working as a children's book illustrator when he became involved in adventure gaming, an interest which eventually led to the creation of several successful games. He is the inventor/illustrator of some of Britain's best-selling fantasy games.

BOOK 7

Castle Death

Joe Dever and Gary Chalk

 Pacer BOOKS FOR YOUNG ADULTS

B

BERKLEY BOOKS, NEW YORK

To all the members of the Lone Wolf Club –
may their endurance never run out!

To Daniel,

it was nice

knowing you

From Aaron Kohli

ACTION CHART

MAGNAKAI DISCIPLINES   NOTES

1	
2	
3	
4	4th Magnakai discipline if you have completed 1 Magnakai adventure successfully

MAGNAKAI LORE - CIRCLE   BONUSES

	CS	EP		CS	EP
CIRCLE OF FIRE	+1	+2	CIRCLE OF SOLARIS	+1	+3
CIRCLE OF LIGHT	0	+3	CIRCLE OF THE SPIRIT	+3	+3

BACKPACK (max. 8 articles)

BACKPACK	MEALS
1	
2	
3	— 3 EP if no Meal available when instructed to eat.
4	
5	BELT POUCH Containing Gold Crowns (50 maximum)
6	
7	
8	

Can be discarded when not in combat.

EP = ENDURANCE POINTS   CS = COMBAT SKILL

COMBAT SKILL	ENDURANCE POINTS
	Can never go above initial score 0 = dead

COMBAT RECORD

ENDURANCE POINTS		ENDURANCE POINTS
LONE WOLF	COMBAT RATIO	ENEMY
LONE WOLF	COMBAT RATIO	ENEMY
LONE WOLF	COMBAT RATIO	ENEMY
LONE WOLF	COMBAT RATIO	ENEMY
LONE WOLF	COMBAT RATIO	ENEMY
MAGNAKAI RANK		

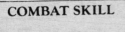

SPECIAL ITEMS LIST

DESCRIPTION	KNOWN EFFECTS

WEAPONS LIST

WEAPONS (maximum 2 Weapons)
1
2

If holding Weapon and appropriate Weaponmastery in combat +2 CS. If combat entered carrying no Weapon —4 CS.

WEAPONMASTERY CHECKLIST

DAGGER		SPEAR	
MACE		SHORT SWORD	
WARHAMMER		BOW	
AXE		SWORD	
QUARTERSTAFF		BROADSWORD	

QUIVER & ARROWS

Quiver	No. of arrows carried
YES/NO	

THE STORY SO FAR . . .

You are the warrior, Lone Wolf, last of the Kai
Masters of Sommerlund and sole survivor of the
massacre that destroyed your kinsmen during a bitter
war with your age-old enemies, the Darklords of
Helgedad.

Many centuries have passed since Sun Eagle, the first
of your kind, established the Order of the Kai. Aided
by the magicians of Dessi, he completed a perilous
quest to find seven crystals of power known as the
Lorestones of Nyxator. With their discovery he
unlocked a wisdom and strength that lay within both
the Lorestones and himself. He recorded the nature
of his discoveries and his experiences in a great tome
called *The Book of the Magnakai*. You have discovered this lost Kai treasure and have given a solemn pledge to restore the Kai to their former glory,
ensuring the security of your land in the years to
come. However, your diligent study of this ancient
book has enabled you to master only three of the ten
Magnakai Disciplines. To fulfil your pledge, you must
complete the quest first undertaken by Sun Eagle
over one thousand years ago. By doing so successfully, you too, will acquire the power and wisdom of
the Magnakai that is held within the Lorestones'
crystal forms.

11

Much of Sun Eagle's script had faded with the passing years and little remained to help you find the seven Lorestones of Nyxator. Guided by the few words that could still be deciphered, you set out upon a journey that took you to the war-torn city of Tekaro in the hostile land of Slovia. There, hidden deep in the crypt of the city's cathedral, you found the first Lorestone of Varetta. As you held the crystal triumphantly in your hand, its power was transfused into your being, and the location of the second stone formed slowly in your mind – Herdos.

The remote township of Herdos stands upon the shore of Lake Khor, high in the Xulun mountains of Dessi. Here the Elder Magi, the magicians who rule the land, helped Sun Eagle on his quest long ago. Time has turned full circle, and once more their aid is sought by a warrior of the Kai.

'Fate has brought you to us, Lone Wolf,' intones Rimoah, speaker for the High Council of the Elder Magi, as you stand before them in the Tower of Truth at Elzian. 'And our fate is bound to your quest.'

His clear voice fills the great cylindrical council chamber and the white-robed elders gathered around you respond with one voice 'It is so.'

Rimoah leads you to a circular dais, set like a deep well into the green marble floor. Carefully, he kneels and touches its liquid metal surface with his gloved hand. A current flows through the shimmering metal and, within its mirror-like depths, a strange vision slowly takes shape. You see a black-walled fortress set upon a rocky isle, its deep purple shadows reflecting in the dark waters of a moonlit lake.

12

You see before you Kazan-Oud. The Lorestone of Herdos rests in this castle, deep within its accursed halls. We will take you to this fortress, Lone Wolf, but you must enter alone, for our powers hold no sway over the forces that command this terrible place. In the years that have passed since Sun Eagle first came to this land, a great evil has consumed Kazan-Oud. We lack the means to destroy this evil but we have laboured to contain it, to prevent it from spreading beyond the Isle of Khor. Some of the bravest warriors of Magnamund have tried at our behest to defeat the power of Kazan-Oud, yet all have perished. But fate now brings us a Kai Master and our hearts rejoice, for the success of your quest will defeat the bane of Kazan-Oud and deliver us all from its evil shadow.'

A ripple of hopeful whispers arises from the circle of Elders when they hear you state that you will go to Kazan-Oud. As they accompany you from the council chamber to equip you for the dangerous mission that lies ahead, you ask the meaning of the words 'Kazan-Oud'. An uneasy silence descends on the dignified company and all eyes turn to Rimoah.

'In the language of the Sommlending,' he says, his voice wavering, 'Castle Death.'

THE GAME RULES

You keep a record of your adventure on the *Action Chart* that you will find in the front of this book. For further adventuring you can copy out the chart yourself or get it photocopied.

During your training as a Kai Master you have developed fighting prowess – COMBAT SKILL and physical stamina – ENDURANCE Before you set off on your adventure you need to measure how effective your training has been. To do this take a pencil and, with your eyes closed, point with the blunt end of it on to the *Random Number Table* on the last page of this book. If you pick *0* it counts as zero.

The first number that you pick from the *Random Number Table* in this way represents your COMBAT SKILL. Add 10 to the number you picked and write the total in the COMBAT SKILL section of your *Action Chart*. (ie, if your pencil fell on the number 4 in the *Random Number Table* you would write in a COMBAT SKILL of 14.) When you fight, your COMBAT SKILL will be pitted against that of your enemy. A high score in this section is therefore very desirable.

The second number that you pick from the *Random Number Table* represents your powers of ENDURANCE. Add 20 to this number and write the total in the

ENDURANCE section of your *Action Chart*. (ie, if your pencil fell on the number 6 on the *Random Number Table* you would have 26 ENDURANCE points.)

If you are wounded in combat you will lose ENDURANCE points. If at any time your ENDURANCE points fall to zero, you are dead and the adventure is over. Lost ENDURANCE points can be regained during the course of the adventure, but your number of ENDURANCE points can never rise above the number you started with.

If you have successfully completed any of the previous adventures in the Lone Wolf series, you can carry your current scores of COMBAT SKILL and ENDURANCE points over to Book 7. You may also carry over any Weapons and Special Items you have in your possession at the end of your last adventure, and these should be entered on your new Action Chart (you are still limited to two Weapons and eight Backpack Items).

You many choose one bonus Magnakai Discipline to add to your Action Chart for every Lone Wolf Magnakai adventure you successfully complete (Books 6 – 12).

MAGNAKAI DISCIPLINES

During your training as a Kai Lord, and in the course of the adventures that led to the discovery of *The Book of the Magnakai*, you have mastered all ten of the basic warrior skills known as the Kai Disciplines.

After studying *The Book of the Magnakai*, you have also reached the rank of Kai Master Superior, which means that you have learnt *three* of the Magnakai Disciplines listed below. It is up to you to choose which three skills these are. As all of the Magnakai Disciplines will be of use to you at some point on your adventure, pick your three with care. The correct use of a Magnakai Discipline at the right time can save your life.

The Magnakai skills are divided into groups, each of which is governed by a separate school of training. These groups are called 'Lore-circles'. By mastering all of the Magnakai Disciplines in a particular Lore-circle, you can gain an increase in your COMBAT SKILL and ENDURANCE points score. (See the section 'Lore-circles of the Magnakai' for details of these bonuses.)

When you have chosen your three Magnakai Disciplines, enter them in the Magnakai Disciplines section of your *Action Chart*.

Weaponmastery

This Magnakai Discipline enables a Kai Master to become proficient in the use of all types of weapon. When you enter combat with a weapon you have mastered, you add 3 points to your COMBAT SKILL. The rank of Kai Master Superior, with which you begin the Magnakai series, means you are skilled in *three* of the weapons in the list below.

SPEAR

DAGGER

MACE

SHORT SWORD

WARHAMMER

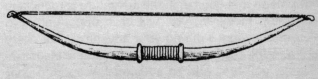

BOW

AXE

SWORD

QUARTERSTAFF

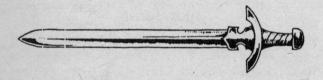

BROADSWORD

The fact that you are skilled with three weapons does not mean that you begin the adventure carrying any of them. However, you will have opportunities to acquire weapons during your adventure. For every Lone Wolf book that you complete in the Magnakai series, you may add an additional weapon to your list.

18

If you choose this skill, write 'Weaponmastery: + 3 COMBAT SKILL points' on your *Action Chart*, and tick your chosen weapons on the weapons list that appears on page 9. You cannot carry more than two weapons.

Animal Control

This Magnakai Discipline enables a Kai Master to communicate with most animals and to determine their purpose and intentions. It also enables a Kai Master to fight from the saddle with great advantage.

If you choose this skill, write 'Animal Control' on your *Action Chart*.

Curing

The possessor of this skill can restore 1 lost ENDURANCE point to his total for every numbered section of the book through which he passes, provided he is not involved in combat. (This can only be done after his ENDURANCE has fallen below its original level.) This Magnakai Discipline also enables a Kai Master to cure disease, blindness and any combat wounds sustained by others, as well as himself. Using the knowledge mastery of this skill provides will also allow a Kai Master to identify the properties of any herbs, roots and potions that may be encountered during the adventure.

If you choose this skill, write 'Curing: + 1 ENDURANCE point for each section without combat' on your *Action Chart*.

Invisibility

This Magnakai skill allows a Kai Master to blend in

with his surroundings, even in the most exposed terrain. It will enable him to mask his body heat and scent, and to adopt the dialect and mannerisms of any town or city that he visits.

If you choose this skill, write 'Invisibility' on your *Action Chart*.

Huntmastery
This skill ensures that a Kai Master will never starve in the wild; he will always be able to hunt for food, even in areas of wasteland and desert. It also enables a Kai Master to move with great speed and dexterity and will allow him to ignore any extra loss of COMBAT SKILL points due to a surprise attack or ambush.

If you choose this skill, write 'Huntmastery' on your *Action Chart*.

Pathsmanship
In addition to the basic skill of being able to recognize the correct path in unknown territory, the Magnakai skill of Pathsmanship will enable a Kai Master to read foreign languages, decipher symbols, read footprints and tracks (even if they have been disturbed), and detect the presence of most traps. It also grants him the gift of always knowing intuitively the position of north.

If you choose this skill, write 'Pathsmanship' on your *Action Chart*.

Psi-surge
This psychic skill enables a Kai Master to attack an enemy using the force of his mind. It can be used as

well as normal combat weapons and adds 4 extra points to your COMBAT SKILL.

It is a powerful Discipline, but it is also a costly one. For every round of combat in which you use Psi-surge, you must deduct 2 ENDURANCE points. A weaker form of Psi-surge called Mindblast can be used against an enemy without losing any ENDURANCE points, but it will add only 2 extra points to your COMBAT SKILL. Psi-surge cannot be used if your ENDURANCE falls to 6 points or below, and not all of the creatures encountered on your adventure will be affected by it; you will be told if a creature is immune.

If you choose this skill, write 'Psi-surge: + 4 COMBAT SKILL points but − 2 ENDURANCE points per round' or 'Mindblast: +2 COMBAT SKILL points' on your *Action Chart*.

Psi-screen
Many of the hostile creatures that inhabit Magnamund have the ability to attack you using their Mindforce. The Magnakai Discipline of Psi-screen prevents you from losing any ENDURANCE points when subjected to this form of attack and greatly increases your defence against supernatural illusions and hypnosis.

If you choose this skill, write 'Psi-screen: no points lost when attacked by Mindforce' on your *Action Chart*.

Nexus
Mastery of this Magnakai skill will enable you to withstand extremes of heat and cold without losing

ENDURANCE points, and to move items by your powers of concentration alone.

If you choose this skill, write 'Nexus' on your *Action Chart*.

Divination
This skill may warn a Kai Master of imminent or unseen danger, or enable him to detect an invisible or hidden enemy. It may also reveal the true purpose or intent of a stranger or strange object encountered in your adventure. Divination may enable you to communicate telepathically with another person and to sense if a creature possesses psychic abilities.

If you choose this skill, write 'Divination' on your *Action Chart*.

If you successfully complete the mission as set in Book 7 of the Lone Wolf Magnakai series, you may add a further Magnakai Discipline of your choice to your *Action Chart* in Book 8. This additional skill, together with your other Magnakai skills and any Special Items that you have found and been able to keep during your adventures, may then be used in the next adventure, which is called *The Jungle of Horrors*.

EQUIPMENT
Before leaving Elzian on your quest for the Lorestone of Herdos, the Elder Magi give you a map of their

land (see inside front cover of this book) and a pouch of gold. To find out how much gold is in the pouch, pick a number from the *Random Number Table*. Add 10 to the number you have picked. The total equals the number of Gold Crowns inside the pouch, and you should now enter this number in the 'Gold Crowns' section of your *Action Chart*. If you have successfully completed books 1–6 of the Lone Wolf adventures, you may add this sum to the total sum of Crowns you already possess. You can carry a maximum of only fifty Crowns, but additional Crowns can be left in safe keeping at your Kai monastery.

The Elder Magi offer you a choice of equipment to aid you on your perilous mission. You can take five items from the list below, again adding to these, if necessary, any you may already possess. However, remember that you can carry a maximum of two Weapons and eight Backpack Items.

SWORD (Weapons)
BOW (Weapons)
QUIVER (Special Items) This contains six arrows. Tick them off as they are used.

ROPE (Backpack Items)

POTION OF LAUMSPUR (Backpack Items) This potion restores 4 ENDURANCE points to your total when swallowed after combat. There is enough for only one dose.

LANTERN (Backpack Items)
MACE (Weapons)

3 MEALS (Meals) Each Meal takes up one space in your Backpack.

DAGGER (Weapons)

3 FIRESEEDS (Special Items.) When thrown against a hard surface, these fireseeds explode and burn fiercely.

List the five items that you choose on your *Action Chart*, under the heading given in brackets, and make a note of any effect they may have on your ENDURANCE points or COMBAT SKILL.

How to carry equipment

Now that you have your equipment, the following list shows you how it is carried. You do not need to make notes but you can refer back to this list in the course of your adventure.

SWORD – carried in the hand.
BOW – carried in the hand.
QUIVER – slung over your shoulder.
ROPE – carried in the Backpack.
POTION OF LAUMSPUR – carried in the Backpack.
LANTERN – carried in the Backpack.
MACE – carried in the hand.
MEALS – carried in the Backpack.
DAGGER – carried in the hand.
FIRESEEDS– carried in your pocket.

How much can you carry?

Weapons
The maximum number of weapons that you may carry is *two*.

Backpack Items
These must be stored in your Backpack. Because space is limited, you may keep a maximum of only eight articles, including Meals, in your Backpack at any one time.

Special Items
Special Items are not carried in the Backpack. When you discover a Special Item, you will be told how to carry it.

Gold Crowns
These are always carried in the Belt Pouch. It will hold a maximum of fifty Crowns.

Food
Food is carried in your Backpack. Each Meal counts as one item.

Any item that may be of use and can be picked up on your adventure and entered on your *Action Chart* is given initial capitals (eg Gold Dagger, Magic Pendant) in the text. Unless you are told it is a Special Item, carry it in your Backpack.

How to use your equipment

Weapons
Weapons aid you in combat. If you have the Magnakai Discipline of Weaponmastery and a correct weapon, it adds 3 points to your COMBAT SKILL. If you enter a combat with no weapons, deduct 4 points from your COMBAT SKILL and fight with your bare hands. If you find a weapon during the adventure, you may pick it up and use it. (Remember that you can only carry *two* weapons at once.)

Bow and Arrows
During your adventure there will be opportunities to use a bow and arrow. If you equip yourself with this weapon, and you possess at least one arrow, you may use it when the text of a particular section allows you to do so. The bow is a useful weapon, for it enables you to hit an enemy at a distance. However, a bow cannot be used in hand-to-hand combat, therefore it is strongly recommended that you also equip yourself with a close combat weapon, like a sword or mace.

In order to use a bow you must possess a quiver and at least one arrow. Each time the bow is used, erase an arrow from your *Action Chart*. A bow cannot, of course, be used if you exhaust your supply of arrows, but the opportunity may arise during your adventure for you to replenish your stock of arrows.

If you have the Magnakai Discipline of Weapon-mastery with a bow, you may add 3 to any number that you choose from the *Random Number Table*, when using the bow. If you enter combat armed only with a bow, you must deduct 4 points from your COMBAT SKILL and fight with your bare hands.

Backpack Items

During your travels you will discover various useful items which you may wish to keep. (Remember you can only carry a maximum of eight items in your Backpack at any time.) You may exchange or discard them at any point when you are not involved in combat.

Special Items

Special Items are not carried in the Backpack. When you discover a Special Item, you will be told how to carry it. If you have successfully completed previous Lone Wolf books, you may already possess Special Items.

Gold Crowns

The currency of Dessi is the Crown, which is a small gold coin. Whenever you kill an enemy and search the body, you may take any Gold Crowns that you find and put them in your Belt Pouch. (Remember the pouch can carry a maximum of fifty Gold Crowns.)

Food

You will need to eat regularly during your adventure. If you do not have any food when you are instructed to eat a Meal, you will lose 3 ENDURANCE points. If you have chosen the Magnakai Discipline of Huntmastery as one of your skills, you will not need to tick off a Meal when instructed to eat.

Potion of Laumspur

This is a healing potion that can restore 4 ENDURANCE points to your total when swallowed after combat. There is enough for one dose only. If you discover any other potion during the adventure, you will be informed of its effect. All potions are Backpack Items.

RULES FOR COMBAT

There will be occasions during your adventure when you have to fight an enemy. The enemy's COMBAT SKILL and ENDURANCE points are given in the text. Lone Wolf's aim in the combat is to kill the enemy by reducing his ENDURANCE points to zero while losing as few ENDURANCE points as possible himself.

At the start of a combat, enter Lone Wolf's and the enemy's ENDURANCE points in the appropriate boxes on the Combat Record section of your *Action Chart*.

The sequence for combat is as follows:

1. Add any extra points gained through your Magnakai Disciplines and Special Items to your current COMBAT SKILL total.

2. Subtract the COMBAT SKILL of your enemy from this total. The result is your *Combat Ratio*. Enter it on the *Action Chart*.

Example

Lone Wolf (COMBAT SKILL 15) is attacked by a Nightstalker (COMBAT SKILL 22). He is not given the opportunity to evade combat, but must stand and fight as the creature leaps on him. Lone Wolf has the Magnakai Discipline of Psi-surge to which the Nightstalker is not immune, so Lone Wolf adds 4 points to his COMBAT SKILL giving a total COMBAT SKILL of 19.

He subtracts the Nightstalker's COMBAT SKILL from his own, giving a *Combat Ratio* of −3. (19 − 22 = −3). −3 is noted on the *Action Chart* as the *Combat Ratio*.

3. When you have your *Combat Ratio*, pick a number from the *Random Number Table*.

4. Turn to the *Combat Results Table* on the inside back cover of the book. Along the top of the chart are shown the *Combat Ratio* numbers. Find the number that is the same as your *Combat Ratio* and cross-reference it with the random number that you have picked (the random numbers appear on the side of the chart). You now have the number of ENDURANCE points lost by both

29

Lone Wolf and his enemy in this round of combat. (*E* represents points lost by the enemy; *LW* represents points lost by Lone Wolf.)

Example

The *Combat Ratio* between Lone Wolf and the Nightstalker has been established as −3. If the number taken from the *Random Number Table* is a 6, then the result of the first round of combat is:

Lone Wolf loses 3 ENDURANCE points (plus an additional 2 points for using Psi-surge)
Nightstalker loses 6 ENDURANCE points

5. On the *Action Chart*, mark the changes in ENDURANCE points to the participants in the combat.

6. Unless otherwise instructed, or unless you have an option to evade, the next round of combat now starts.

7. Repeat the sequence from Stage 3.

This process of combat continues until the ENDURANCE points of either the enemy or Lone Wolf are reduced to zero, at which point the one with the zero score is declared dead. If Lone Wolf is dead, the adventure is over. If the enemy is dead, Lone Wolf proceeds but with his ENDURANCE points reduced.

A summary of Combat Rules appears on the page after the *Random Number Table*.

Evasion of combat

During your adventure you may be given the chance to evade combat. If you have already engaged in a round of combat and decide to evade, calculate the combat for that round in the usual manner. All points lost by the enemy as a result of that round are ignored, and you make your escape. Only Lone Wolf may lose ENDURANCE points during that round, but then that is the risk of running away! You may only evade if the text of the particular section allows you to do so.

LEVELS OF MAGNAKAI TRAINING

The following table is a guide to the rank and titles that are achieved by Kai Masters at each stage of their training. As you successfully complete each adventure in the *Lone Wolf* Magnakai series, you will gain an additional Magnakai Discipline and progress towards the ultimate distinction of a Kai Warrior – Kai Grand Mastership.

No. of Magnakai Disciplines mastered by Kai Master	Magnakai Rank
1	Kai Master
2	Kai Master Senior
3	Kai Master Superior – *You begin the Lone Wolf Magnakai adventures with this level of training*
4	Primate
5	Tutelary
6	Principalin
7	Mentora
8	Scion-kai
9	Archmaster
10	Kai Grand Master

LORE-CIRCLES OF THE MAGNAKAI

In the years before their massacre, the Kai Masters of Sommerlund devoted themselves to the study of the Magnakai. These skills were divided into four schools of training called 'Lore-circles'. By mastering all of the Magnakai Disciplines of a Lore-circle, the Kai Masters developed their fighting prowess (COMBAT SKILL), and their physical and mental stamina (ENDURANCE) to a level far higher than any mortal warrior could otherwise attain.

Listed below are the four Lore-circles of the Magnakai and the skills that must be mastered in order to complete them.

Title of Magnakai Lore-circle	Magnakai Disciplines needed to complete the Lore-circle
CIRCLE OF FIRE	Weaponmastery & Huntmastery
CIRCLE OF LIGHT	Animal control & Curing
CIRCLE OF SOLARIS	Invisiblity, Huntmastery & Pathsmanship
CIRCLE OF THE SPIRIT	Psi-surge, Psi-shield, Nexus & Divination

33

By completing a Lore-circle, you may add to your COMBAT SKILL and ENDURANCE the extra bonus points that are shown below.

Lore-circle bonuses

	COMBAT SKILL	ENDURANCE
CIRCLE OF FIRE	+1	+2
CIRCLE OF LIGHT	0	+3
CIRCLE OF SOLARIS	+1	+3
CIRCLE OF THE SPIRIT	+3	+3

All bonus points that you acquire by completing a Lore-circle are additions to your basic COMBAT SKILL and ENDURANCE scores.

IMPROVED DISCIPLINES

As you rise through the higher levels of Magnakai training you will find that some of your skills will steadily improve. If you are a Kai Master that has reached the rank of Primate, you will now benefit from improvements to the following Magnakai Disciplines:

Animal Control
Primates with this Magnakai Discipline will be able to repel an animal that is intent on harming them by blocking its sense of taste and smell. The level of success is dependent on the size and ferocity of the animal.

Curing
Primates with this skill will have the ability to delay the effects of poisons, including venoms, that they may come into contact with. Although a Kai Primate with this skill will not be able to neutralize a poison he will be able to slow its effect, giving him more time to find an antidote or cure.

Huntmastery
Primates with this skill will have a greatly increased agility and be able to climb without the use of climbing aids, such as ropes, etc.

Psi-surge
Primates with the Magnakai Discipline of Psi-surge will, by concentrating their psychic powers upon an

object, be able to set up vibrations that may lead to the disruption or destruction of the object.

Nexus
Primates with the skill of Nexus will be able to offer a far greater resistance than before to the effects of noxious gases and fumes.

The nature of any additional improvements and how they affect your Magnakai Disciplines will be noted in the Improved Disciplines section of future Lone Wolf books.

MAGNAKAI WISDOM

Your quest for the Lorestone of Herdos will be fraught with danger for the fortress of Kazan-Oud has a dark and sinister reputation for being the ruin of many a brave adventurer. Make notes as you progress through the story – they will be of great help in this and future adventures.

Many things that you find will help you during your adventure. Some Special Items will be of use in future Lone Wolf adventures and others may be red herrings of no real use at all, so be selective in what you decide to keep.

Choose your three Magnakai Disciplines with care, for a wise choice enables any player to complete the quest, no matter how weak his initial COMBAT SKILL and ENDURANCE points scores. Successful completion of previous Lone Wolf adventures, although an advantage, is not essential for the completion of this Magnakai adventure.

May the spirit of your ancestors guide you on the path of the Magnakai.

Good luck!

The hours leading up to your departure from Elzian are spent checking and double-checking your equipment and provisions. But, no matter how hard you try to concentrate on these preparations, your mind is constantly invaded by the shadowy image of Kazan-Oud, an image identical to the vision that appeared the previous evening in the well of the council chamber. You are filled with a deep dread, as you contemplate the probable site of your own grave. However, coupled to this terrible sense of foreboding is a far greater and irresistible desire to discover the Lorestone of Herdos.

Shortly before dawn, your thoughts are disturbed by a knock at the door of your chamber: it is Rimoah. The time has come for your mission to begin. You follow him through halls and galleries to a rooftop platform nestling among the crimson towers of the Temple of Truth. Here you are greeted by a young man. He is tall and dark-sknned, with plaited flaxen hair and sharp, cat-like eyes, and he wears the gold and scarlet tunic of a Vakeros – a warrior-magician of Dessi. 'Hail, Paido!' says Rimoah, bowing to this proud young man.

'Hail, my Lord Rimoah,' he replies, respectfully. 'We are ready to sail.'

The first rays of the dawn light shimmer along the golden hull of a magnificent sky-ship that hovers above the rooftop platform. As the hum of its powerful engine rises, you thank Rimoah and bid him farewell before following Lord Paido to the boarding ladder at the edge of the platform. Once safely on board, the sky-ship rises into the chill dawn air and Lord Rimoah and the Tower of Truth shrink swiftly beneath its golden keel. You look down with growing fascination as the sleek, bat-winged craft passes over the circling waters of the Elzian Canal, and speeds northwards above the jungle of central Dessi. As the grey chasm of Gorgoron looms into view, splitting the emerald-green land like a deep and terrible wound, Lord Paido joins you at the rail. Time passes in conversation and you learn much about the people of this untamed land and their history. You learn that the Elder Magi are all that remain of a race of great magicians who ruled central Magnamund many thousands of years ago. They were wise and powerful and their leadership was great until their numbers were decimated by a plague that swept across the world. Those who survived sought refuge in Dessi and have lived here, in the mountains and the jungle, ever since. The Vakeros are native soldiers of Dessi who have been taught the art of battle-magic by the Elder Magi to help them defend the northern border against invasion by the war-like Vassagonians.

When you tell Lord Paido of your own past battles with the desert warriors, you sense a sadness within him. 'How I wish my brother Kasin were here with us now,' he says, staring thoughtfully towards the distant horizon. 'He could tell many a brave tale of the great desert wars.' You ask what has become of his brother. There is a long pause before he replies solemnly: 'Kazan-Oud.'

The land of Dessi is now spread out beneath you like a gigantic map. To the north-west you can see the foothills of the Carcos range and a faint ribbon-like glimmer that is the River Doi; to the east, a bank of grey stormclouds advances unchecked across a sea of jungle vegetation. Shortly before noon you sight your destination. The low-domed buildings of Herdos appear on the horizon, followed by the waters of Lake Khor and a blackened finger of rock upon which sits Kazan-Oud. Even at this great distance, the awesome sight of the terrible fortress sends a chill along your spine.

Lord Paido orders his crew to prepare for landing and, within the hour, the great sky-ship is casting its shadow upon the flagstones of the Plaza of Herdos. You are welcomed by Lord Ardan, Elder of Herdos, and a detachment of his Vakeros guards. They escort you through the streets of the ancient town, past the tiny stone-walled dwellings of fishermen and miners, to a quay where a glass-domed tower several storeys high commands access to the busy harbour. As you enter the tower, you notice that the glass dome radiates a greenish light that, in spite of the blinding glare of the midday sun, can be seen quite clearly.

Later, as the sun sinks slowly behind the peaks of the Xulun mountains, the light emanating from the tower becomes more visible covering Lake Khor with an umbrella of ghostly luminescence. Lord Ardan explains: 'This tower, together with five others that encircle the lake, generates a shield of magical energy that imprisons the evil of Kazan-Oud. No creature, living or dead, can enter or leave the Isle of Khor so long as our shield remains intact. We dare not lower our guard, and, to allow you to land on the island, we have devised a means by which you may pass through the shield unharmed.' He takes a gem the size of a small apple from the pocket of his silken robe and places it in your hand. It is a dull transluscent red, but within its core a swirling mist of glittering sparks flickers with gold and silver fire.

'It is a Power-key. Guard it well, for so long as you possess it you may fulfil your quest; lose it and you will never escape from the Isle of Khor.' (Mark the Power-key on your *Action Chart* as a Special Item, which you carry in the pocket of your tunic.) 'At midnight, my Vakeros will take you by boat to the edge of the shield. On board is a small coracle in which you can pass through the shield and make your way to the Isle of Khor. We shall pray for you, Lone Wolf.'

Midnight finds you standing on the deck of a square-rigged fishing boat. The sighing night wind and the creak of rope and timber are the only sounds that accompany you across the black waters of Lake Khor. You arrive at a wall of shimmering green light: the power-shield. The Vakeros whisper their good-byes and you paddle through the wall, drawing closer with every stroke to the sinister island fortress.

Two hundred yards from the glistening black shore-line, you note two places where you can make a landing.

If you wish to land at a stone jetty to the west of Kazan-Oud, turn to **135**.

If you wish to land at a sheltered bay to the east of Kazan-Oud, turn to **288**.

2

Your eye is drawn to a panel on the hexagonal wall. The central part of the stonework is much newer than the surrounding edges, a detail which your Kai Discipline enabled you to recognize at a glance. After closer examination, you are sure that there was once a door in this wall. The stone does not sound as if it is solid when you tap it and you suspect it would not withstand several well-placed blows.

If you wish to try to break through the wall, turn to **228**.

If you do not wish to break through the wall, you can still enter the ruby corridor; turn to **349**.

Or, you can enter the jadin corridor; turn to **163**.

3

The rumble of a massive counterweight descending behind the wall sends a shudder through the flagstones. The portcullis rises and you hear the lever click back to its original position as you duck under the pointed bars.

Turn to **277**.

4

Your lungs are close to bursting point when your persistance finally pays off. The lock clicks and the door is forced wide open by the sheer weight of the water pressing upon it.

Turn to **172**.

5

The shadow flares red before dissolving into a dense grey mist that is carried away swiftly on the stormy air. A sudden chill makes you shiver. You pull your cloak around you, taking comfort from its warmth, but it is as if the cold comes not from the damp wind but from somewhere deep inside you.

You feel hungry and you must now eat a Meal or lose 3 ENDURANCE points. When you have finished, you make a quick check of your equipment before taking your first cautious steps inside the Great Hall.

Turn to **293**.

6

'Good!' booms the voice of Zahda, as you land on the opposite side of the pit. 'You are brave! But have you brains as well as battle-brawn, I wonder? Ha! Soon we shall see.'

The voice conjures an image of Lord Zahda in your mind. He is seated on a golden throne with the object of your quest, the Lorestone of Herdos, suspended in the air above him. You resolve to survive this accursed maze and escape. If you can then only find your way back to Zahda's throne hall, the success of your quest will be within your grasp.

You walk along the passage that leads away from the pit, your mind filled with dismay as you contemplate the problems and perils that lie before you. One such problem looms into view as the passage takes a sharp turn.

Turn to **100**.

7

To your horror, you discover that the quiver is completely empty. Your arrows have fallen out and now lie buried in the nest of vegetation upon which you awoke (erase these arrows from your *Action Chart*).

With a cry of frustration, you discard your bow and unsheathe a hand weapon as the snake draws itself back in preparation to strike.

Turn to **301**.

8

As it springs out of the gloom, you hack at the beast, carving a slice from its great hairy shoulder. But the shock of its attack sends you reeling to the floor, and you scream out in pained surprise. Claws rake your arm; burning saliva stings your face. Desperately, you stab at the snarling beast as it dips its head and closes its massive jaws around your legs. The creature is immune to Mindblast but *not* Psi-surge.

Hound of Death: COMBAT SKILL 22   ENDURANCE 40

If you win the combat, turn to **194**.

9

A faint rumble grows louder. There is a clatter of chains and the squeal of metal on metal as the portcullis rises jerkily into the roof. Wasting no time, you duck under the spiked bars and hurry into the tunnel beyond.

Turn to **277**.

10

Grabbing a Fireseed from the pocket of your tunic, you hurl it at the monster's gaping mouth. It disappears from view and, for a brief moment, you feel the tendril tremble and slacken its crushing grip. Erase one Fireseed from your *Action Chart*.

Turn to **170**.

11

Descending the narrow staircase, you arrive at a tunnel-like corridor, sandwiched between two walls of mouldering masonry. Foul, oily water gurgles along a channel in the slippery floor towards a distant archway, which is blocked by a black, iron portcullis. Bolted to the criss-crossed bars is a plaque which bears a curious design:

On the wall to your left is a large, rusty dial with a brass pointer. Set around it, like the numerals of a clock, are the numbers 1 to 40, and below the dial is a lever. Your basic Kai instincts tell you that by selecting the correct number, or numbers, and pulling the lever, you will open the portcullis.

If you have the Magnakai Discipline of Divination, turn to **167**.

If you have the Magnakai Discipline of Pathsmanship, turn to **306**.

If you have neither of these skills, turn to **329**.

12

'We're as good as dead if we stay here,' says the warrior in a broad Stornlands accent. 'Come, we best find ourselves a safe tunnel before they release a Trakka. We'll have a horde of Zahda's pets snappin' at our heels if it picks up our scent.'

You follow the man through a labyrinth of tunnels and chambers, descending by slope and staircase to deeper levels of this subterranean world. Not a word is spoken until, finally, you stop to rest in a small, musty chamber; its entrance is partially hidden behind a rockfall of scarlet stone. 'How long have you been tunnel-running?' your companion asks. When you reply that you've been in Kazan-Oud no more than a few hours, his face registers a look of surprise followed by disappointment. 'I'd have stood and fought the Dhax had I known I was so near to the surface,' he says, shaking his head and staring dejectedly at the floor.

He tells you that his name is Tavig and that he comes from Suentina, a city in the western land of Slovia.

13

Over a year ago his sister was captured by Sadzar, the slaver of Gzor, when a ship on which she was a passenger was attacked by his pirate fleet off the island of Lipo. One thousand Crowns was the ransom Sadzar placed on her head and Tavig vowed he would raise the gold and save his sister or die in the attempt. Undaunted by the rumours he had heard, he travelled to Herdos to offer his services to the Elder Magi, to attempt the destruction of the evil that haunts Kazan-Oud, in return for his sister's ransom. They agreed to his price, as they had agreed to scores of others' before him, and sent him through the power-shield with their hopes and prayers for success. That was one year ago.

'One man alone could never hope to destroy Zahda, he who commands this fortress, for his power has grown greater than the Elders imagine. I tried and I failed. Twice I've been captured and twice I've escaped from his maze, and now my only wish is to escape from this fortress of nightmares. I'm a tunnel-runner, a survivor, a fugitive from Zahda's law, but I fear my time has nearly run out.'

Drawing his sword, Tavig walks to the entrance and peers into the corridor outside. 'Luck be on your side, stranger,' he says, and hurries away. You call out for him to wait, to tell you more of what he has learnt of Kazan-Oud, but your pleas go unanswered as he disappears into the tunnel.

If you wish to follow him, turn to **119**.
If you decide to continue alone, turn to **308**.

13 – *Illustration I*

The shriek of metal on metal reverberates along the

I. Halfway down the stairs you disturb a colony of bats nesting in the ceiling

14

tunnel as great iron cogs grind into action. Slowly, the portcullis rises into the roof. Wasting no time, you duck beneath the pointed bars and hurry into the passage beyond.

Rats flee, squeaking, as you stalk along the slippery flatstones. You wince as their claws rasp on the wet rock and their hairless tails furrow the stinking green slime that covers the surface of the tunnel floor. The passage widens as it approaches a staircase that leads down. Halfway down the stairs you disturb a colony of bats nesting in the ceiling. They squeal angrily and whirl around your head, battering you with their wings and nipping at your face with their sharp, needle-like teeth.

If you have the Magnakai Discipline of Animal Control or Psi-surge, turn to **180**.

If you have neither of these skills, turn to **285**.

14

The brick slides in and the secret door slides open. Before you stands an ugly bearded dwarf, wearing a grimy black velvet jerkin. His pig-eyes twinkle malevolently as he raises a hollow brass tube and points it at your face.

'Sweetdreams,' he cackles, and a blast of icy-cold vapour shoots from the tip, catching you squarely in the face. You reel back, coughing and choking as the bitter vapour fills your lungs. By the time you realize that you have inhaled a powerful sleep gas, your body is already succumbing to its irresistible power.

Turn to **165**.

15

You spin a screw-like handle set in the centre of the door, releasing the lock. You open the door and enter: inside, you discover a room of steel. The walls, ceiling and floor are all constructed of metal plate, which is polished to give a mirror-like shine. Low, iron tables are set out with the implements and accessories of magic: crucibles, retorts, aludels, flasks and all manner of twisting glass tubes, which bubble and seethe with multi-coloured liquids. Vellum-bound tomes and crumbling parchments litter the shelves, competing for space with repulsive-looking pink organs floating in glass jars of vile-smelling preservative. Quickly you scan the shelves in search of useful items and, to your delight, rediscover all your confiscated weapons. (Re-enter on your *Action Chart* everything that was taken from you before you were sent to the maze.)

In addition to your weapons, you discover a large jar of concentrated Laumspur (restores 8 ENDURANCE points), and a Platinum Amulet. If you wish to take the Amulet, mark it on your *Action Chart* as a Special Item, which you wear on your wrist. It will protect you from injury due to exposure to high temperatures.

Elated by the rediscovery of your equipment, you leave the chamber and press on along the shiny steel tube.

Turn to **90**.

16

It takes a few minutes for you to get your bearings in the gloom of the narrow corridor. Outside, strange sounds echo across the beach, making you forget your natural caution and move deeper into the darkness. The uneven floor is coated with mud, and the warm, moist air reeks with a repugnant odour that reminds you of gutted fish. You press on, taking great pains not to slip and fall but the light soon fades completely and you slow to a halt.

If you possess a Kalte Firesphere, a Lantern or a Torch and Tinderbox, turn to **61**.

If you do not possess any of these Items, turn to **277**.

17

A movement at the end of the corridor warns you that more guards are entering the sarcophagus, alerted no doubt by the noise of combat. Rather than be caught without cover in this narrow corridor, you decide to enter the chamber and attempt to escape along the opposite passage.

Turn to **69**.

18

With the words of the skull reverberating in your mind, you pull out the cork with your teeth and shake the liquid into the pit, spreading it in a wide arc from left to right. You are certain that there is an invisible bridge across the pit; if only you could locate it.

The footsteps halt. You hear a piercing crack, like that of a whip, and, immediately afterwards, an angry red weal opens around your wrist (lose 2 ENDURANCE points). The container spins from your hand and seems to bounce in mid-air before dropping into the void. You have found the bridge! But now you have an invisible enemy to contend with.

If you wish to step on to the invisible bridge, turn to **166**.

If you wish to fight your unseen enemy, turn to **257**.

19

A shadow crosses your path and you release the bow string, but your arrow does not find its mark. A ghoulish howl is the only warning you receive before the creatures leap out of the billowing smoke, clawing and biting at your face and arms.

Dhax: COMBAT SKILL 25   ENDURANCE 32

Unless you have the Magnakai Discipline of Hunt-mastery, deduct 3 points from your COMBAT SKILL for the first two rounds of combat, due to the speed and surprise of your enemy's attack.

You may evade combat after three rounds by running into the archway opposite; turn to **241**.

If you win combat, turn to **141**.

20

The passage leads to an enormous compound of cells that holds the slaves of Kazan-Oud. They are, in the main, a pitiful herd of gangling, black-skinned creatures, with sorrowful eyes and backs bent crooked by years of hard labour. These prisoners press their sad faces against the tiny grates of their cells, curious to see the fair-skinned warrior who walks upright among them.

They hiss as you pass until the entire complex echoes to the sound of their sibilent scorn. At the end of the block, there is a cell that resembles a cage, denying its prisoner even the small degree of privacy provided by the others. You stare through the bars at a dark-skinned man sleeping on the straw-covered floor. His blond hair and red and gold tunic are stained with blood and grime. A key to his cell hangs by a cord on a peg driven into the nearby wall.

If you wish to take the key and release him, turn to **113**.

If you prefer to leave him and continue, turn to **142**.

21

A maniacal scream of anger echoes from behind the grating as the giant snake crashes lifelessly to the ground. Suddenly bolts of red fire are raining down all around you, splintering the stone floor and leaving nothing but molten cinders wherever they strike. You clamber across the snake and dive into the tunnel to avoid this rain of crimson death.

To your dismay, you discover the tunnel is no more

than a shallow cave, a shelter for a clutch of eggs, each one no smaller than a barrel of ale. They rest upon a bed of packs and torn clothing, the last remains of adventurers who fell foul of the traps of Kazan-Oud.

If you wish to examine these items more closely, turn to **148**.

If you wish to look for a way of escape from this tunnel, turn to **346**.

22

The Rahkos lies motionless on the ground before you but, in spite of the many blows you have dealt the creature, it bears no sign of having ever been involved in combat.

If you wish to turn your back on the hand and enter the passage ahead, turn to **77**.

If you wish to take a closer look at the hand, turn to **215**.

23

The stone blocks of a fallen tower lie scattered in an uneven line across the beach, like the vertebrae of a long dead giant. Lightning flashes and you see in the battlements of Kazan-Oud a wide breach in the wall where the tower once stood. A stone staircase rises from the beach to the top of the ruined wall, but sections of it are missing, presumably torn away when the tower collapsed.

If you wish to attempt to climb the stairs to the fortess, turn to **150**.

If you prefer to continue along the beach, turn to **348**.

24

After what seems like an hour, but in reality is only a few minutes at the most, the scorching heat subsides and the tunnel air becomes painless to breathe. You press on and soon arrive at an archway, where the shiny steel tube enters a chamber gouged out of solid black iron. There a spiral staircase ascends to a portal. You climb the stairs and peer out through the portal. A sight greets you that sets your pulse racing. Before you stands a gleaming block of solid gold – the back of Lord Zahda's throne. Above it, hovering motionless in the air, are two perfect crystals: one glows darkly with black fire; the other radiates a pure golden light that sends a shiver down your spine. It is the object of your quest – the Lorestone of Herdos.

If you wish to reach up and take the Lorestone, turn to **42**.

If you wish to attack the black crystal, turn to **138**.

If you prefer to examine the throne, turn to **98**.

25

Your senses scream a warning that this object is evil. A powerful spell of shielding has been placed upon it to conceal its true purpose, but your mastery of the psychic disciplines helps you to overcome this barrier. It is a means by which its sorcerous creator may exert his control over any who touch it or gaze upon it.

A coldness probes your mind, like fingers of ice seeking to crush your will, but your Psi-screen melts the numbing grip of this psychic attack. You lash out with your foot and send the Sceptre spinning into the chasm. There is a silence, then a dull boom, like distant thunder, reverberates in the abyss far below.

If you now wish to enter the east tunnel, from which the Dhax appeared, turn to **185**.

If you prefer to enter the west tunnel, turn to **308**.

26

The inner surface of the bubble is lined with globules of transparent fat, which absorb the force of your blows.

Pick a number from the *Random Number Table* and add 3 to the number you have picked. If you have the Magnakai Discipline of Weaponskill with sword, deduct 2 from this figure. The final number equals the number of ENDURANCE points you lose owing to lack of oxygen before you cut your way free from the transparent prison.

If you survive the ordeal, you can cut your way through the rest of the bubbles; turn to **151**.

27 – *Illustration II (overleaf)*

Stepping carefully through the slime-smeared rubble, you stop for a moment to catch your breath and survey the shattered keep of Kazan-Oud. It is a desolate sight. Only stone buildings remain intact and everything is covered with creepers and mildew. A great fire must have ravaged the inner fortress to have resulted in such total devastation.

In the centre of the keep stands the Great Hall, still an imposing stronghold and made all the more frightening by the constant flash of green lightning. Beyond its burnt and fungus-covered wooden door, twisted

11.   A shadowy figure with flaming red eyes is hovering in the sky, its hand gripping a great spiked ball and chain

tree forms, with sharp, barbed thorns, sprawl across the cracked flagstones like coils of steel wire. You are about to enter when a movement in the air around your head arrests you. A shape is taking form in the doorway, a shadowy figure with flaming red eyes. An icy chill grips your heart as it sweeps past you with a swirling rush of wind. You spin round to see it hovering in the sky, its shadowy hand now gripping a great spiked ball and chain. It shrieks an unearthly cry and the ball whistles down towards your unprotected face.

If you have the Magnakai Discipline of Psi-screen, turn to **38**.

If you do not possess this skill, you must prepare to defend yourself, for there is no time to evade this sudden attack. Owing to the speed of the attack, deduct 3 points from your COMBAT SKILL total for the first three rounds of combat (unless you have the Magnakai Discipline of Huntmastery).

Oudakon: COMBAT SKILL 20   ENDURANCE 29

If you win the combat, turn to **5**.

28

Before you reach his body, a second crossbow bolt hits your head. The missile passes through your skull and you are dead before your body hits the ground.

Your life and your quest end here.

29

The tunnel winds its way deeper and deeper into the solid rock until it emerges at a chamber illuminated by a shaft of shimmering red light that pours down from a square hole in the ceiling. A pair of huge iron doors fills the opposite wall and appears to offer the only exit from the room. In order to reach the doors, you will have to pass through the eerie red light.

> If you wish to walk through the light and examine the iron doors, turn to **269**.
>
> If you prefer to retrace your steps and take the east tunnel, turn to **272**.

30

The sand is unexpectedly warm and, as you make your way between the boulders that litter the shore, your boots soon become unbearably hot. Just a few feet ahead, a distinct line of stepping stones rises out of the sand and heads towards a fissure in the sheer rock wall.

> If you wish to leap on to the nearest stone slab, turn to **177**.
>
> If you choose to avoid the stepping stones and press on through the scorching sand, turn to **104**.

31

Your attack is swift and deadly. You despatch all three of them in as many blows and cover their dead bodies with a tapestry torn from the wall. There is nothing of value in the pockets of their robes but, lying on the table, you find a Skeleton Key and a Parchment. Both Items look as if they could be of use and you decide to keep them. (Mark them as Special Items on your *Action Chart*, to be kept in the pocket of your tunic.)

You leave the chamber but, as soon as you set foot into the corridor beyond, you are confronted by an armoured guard. He screams a cry that is muffled by the visor of his helmet, and turns to run towards a bell-rope hanging from a hole in the ceiling.

If you have a bow and wish to use it, turn to **266**.
If you do not have a bow, or do not wish to use it, turn to **40**.

32

As the tip of your weapon flicks the lever down, you feel a surge of water engulf your arm. The flow is reversed: the statue is sucking water from the chamber at a tremendous rate. Your weapon is torn from your hand (remember to erase it from your *Action Chart*) but you manage to wrench your arm clear and swim to the surface uninjured.

Within minutes, the water drops to the level of the statue's mouth and remains there. Suddenly, the door emits a click and is forced wide open by the weight of the remaining water pressing upon it.

Turn to **172**.

33

At first there is silence. Then a faint squeak grows to a shuddering rumble as the cogs of a hidden counter-weight grind into action. The squeal of tortured metal resounds in your ears as the portcullis rises jerkily into the soot-blackened ceiling.

Wasting no time you duck under the rising bars and hurry into the tunnel beyond.

Turn to **277**.

In reply to your correct answer, the oval door emits a click and slowly swings open. You step through and descend a steep ramp to a long corridor, whose walls are covered with what appear to be gigantic cocoons that stretch into the distance for as far as you can see. The oval door clicks shut but the clicking continues, like an echo, only growing steadily louder. In the gloomy corridor ahead you can see that something is moving. A huge worm-like creature with great black eyes and horny mandibles is slithering towards you, a purple froth bubbling from its mouth as it picks up your scent.

If you have the Magnakai Discipline of Invisibility, turn to **86**.

If you have the Magnakai Discipline of Animal Kinship and have reached the Kai rank of Primate, turn to **130**.

If you have a Silver Whistle, turn to **347**.

If you have neither of these skills nor the Special Item, turn to **233**.

35

By sheer force of will, you focus your skill through the pain that fills your head, and try to command the sphere to stop its psychic attack.

Pick a number from the *Random Number Table*. If you have reached the Magnakai rank of Primate, you may add 1 to the number you have picked.

If your total is now *0–4*, turn to **97**.
If it is 5 or more, turn to **246**.

36

An opening to your right reveals a spiral staircase and you can distinctly hear the sound of approaching footsteps. Judging by the noise, you estimate that at least a dozen iron-shod warriors are descending the stairs to this level.

If you wish to stand and face the approaching enemy, turn to **273**.
If you wish to descend the stairs as quickly as possible, turn to **55**.

37

In a matter of seconds, the exit is sealed off completely. A loud hissing fills your ears, and a strangely bitter smell assails your nostrils. By the time you realize that the air is being flooded with a powerful sleep gas, pumped in through tiny vents near the floor, you are already succumbing to its irresistible power.

Turn to **165**.

38

Your psychic senses tell you that what you see before you is an illusion. The Oudakon is a spectral force, placed here by a powerful magician and activated by anyone or anything that dares to approach the door of the Great Hall.

Mustering your courage, you challenge the illusion by commanding it to disperse. The shadow, which, seconds before, looked all too real, dissolves like mist into the chill night air. All that remains is a fading cry of frustrated anger that echoes through the ruins of the keep.

Turn to **293**.

39

You sense that a bridge, hidden by a powerful spell of invisibility, spans the pit. Kneeling at the edge, you sweep your hand back and forth in the hope of locating it, but a noise in the passage behind makes you stop and turn. The sound of heavy footsteps grows louder but the passage looks deserted. Frantically, you continue your search for the invisible bridge.

Pick a number from the *Random Number Table*.

If the number you have picked is *0–4*, turn to **344**.
If it is *5–9*, turn to **58**.

40

The guard tugs the rope and the corridor is filled with the harsh clangour of an alarm bell. More armoured guards appear, their weapons drawn and their visors closed for combat. They take one look at you and hurl themselves along the corridor in a frenzied attack. They strike simultaneously and you must fight all four of them as one enemy.

Zahda Beastmen: COMBAT SKILL 30   ENDURANCE 39

If you win and combat lasts three rounds or less, turn to **248**.
If combat lasts more than three rounds, turn to **160**.

41

A terrible growling follows you across the bleak shore as you race towards the high rock wall that is the base of Kazan-Oud. At first the sand felt comfortably warm but now your boots have become unbearably hot.

A few yards ahead, a line of stepping stones rises out of the scorching black sand. The stones lead away towards a jagged fissure in the rock wall.

If you wish to leap on to the nearest stone slab, turn to **177**.
If you choose to avoid the stepping stones and press on through the burning sand, turn to **104**.

42

Your heart pounding, you reach for the Lorestone, your fingers trembling in anticipation of the moment when, by merely touching its crystal shell, you will absorb its vast wisdom. You feel giddy with excitement as your hand draws closer. Then suddenly a severe pain burns your fingers, jolting you to your senses: a gout of black fire has sprung from the dark crystal, stabbing you viciously with its spiky flame (lose 3 ENDURANCE points). Lightning dances around the crystal, fusing it to the Lorestone with a crackling fire. A cone of light bathes the throne and, in its shadowless glare, Lord Zahda appears, gaunt and wild-eyed; in his hand he holds a rod of inlaid platinum, which he now points directly at your head.

If you possess the Sommerswerd, turn to **174**.
If you do not have this Special Item, turn to **202**.

43

The Blue Pills are made from the dried and crushed roots of the Sabito plant, commonly found in the Boari jungle, but rare in any other part of Magnamund. They enable the human body to extract oxygen from water by absorbing it through the skin, thereby allowing anyone who swallows Sabito root to 'breathe' underwater.

There are enough pills for one full dose.

Turn to **323**.

44

Your bleeding hand strikes something close to the edge of the pit that feels like a narrow plank. You thank your good fortune, but before you can scramble across it, a blow catches you in the ribs and leaves you gasping for air (lose 3 ENDURANCE points). You have been dealt a vicious kick that leaves you sprawled over the edge of the pit.

If you wish to get to your feet and try to retaliate, turn to **257**.

If you wish to pull yourself on to the invisible beam and try to struggle across to the other side, turn to **166**.

If you wish to risk diving into the pit, turn to **275**.

45 – *Illustration III (overleaf)*

Unsheathing your weapon, you dig your heels into the wet sand and face the seething tide of rats. The damp air is now filled with the choking stench of their bodies, and your stomach knots as they scuttle nearer and nearer.

If you have completed the Magnakai Lore-circle of Light (ie, you possess the Disciplines of Animal Control and Curing), you may add an additional 2 points to your COMBAT SKILL for the duration of this fight.

Flood of Giant Rats:
COMBAT SKILL 15   ENDURANCE 80

You can evade after three rounds of combat by climbing over the reef of jagged rocks; turn to **336**.

If you win the combat, turn to **283**.

46

The passage opens out into a hexagonal chamber. There are two exits, both leading away beneath

III. You dig your heels into the wet sand and face the seething tide of rats

horseshoe arches of gleaming crystal. The arch to your left is carved from solid red ruby; the arch to your right, from solid green jadin.

> If you wish to pass under the red ruby arch, turn to **349**.
>
> If you wish to pass under the green jadin arch, turn to **163**.
>
> If you have the Magnakai Disciplines of Invisibility, Pathsmanship or Divination, turn to **2**.

47

You are ten feet from the archway when a ghastly scream freezes you in your tracks, and forces you to glance over your shoulder at a terrible scene. Three creatures, no taller than men but with shiny skin as black as night, claw at the warrior in a grisly tug-of-war. The snapping of bone and tearing of flesh makes you shudder, and the sight of the dead man's limbs being swallowed whole makes your stomach churn uncontrollably. The ghoulish creatures gurgle their delight, their jaws dislocating to accommodate their feast. As their fiery eyes fix themselves on you, a cold dagger of fear stabs into your mind. Blinded by panic, you turn and flee into the darkness of the archway.

Turn to **277**.

48

You have barely covered a hundred yards, when a blood-curling howl echoes along the passage behind you. Spinning round, you see the outline of a gigantic black wolf loping towards you at a frightening pace. Its evil eyes flash in the dim light and its great fanged jaws hang open in eager readiness to bite.

If you wish to stand and fight this ravenous monster, turn to **78**.

If you wish to run from the monster as fast as you can, turn to **287**.

49

As the glow of your light fills the cave, you notice that the uneven floor is covered with chunks of mouldering rubble, spattered with blotches of dried blood. You are about to investigate a narrow tunnel that winds deeper into the solid black rock, when your Kai instincts alert you to a shallow step that crosses from one side of the cave to the other. A closer look reveals the step to be a perfect square of marble that covers the first ten feet of the tunnel floor.

If you wish to prod the marble slab with a weapon to test for a trap, turn to **183**.

If you wish to jump across the slab into the tunnel beyond, turn to **127**.

If you decide to enter the tunnel by walking across the slab, turn to **277**.

50

Your arrow strikes its mark, burying itself deep in the chest of the leader. He screams like an animal and falls forward, impaling himself on his sword as he crashes to the ground. Dropping your bow, you draw a hand weapon as the other guards press on with their attack, undaunted by the death of their leader.

Zahda Beastmen:
COMBAT SKILL 28   ENDURANCE 35

If you win the combat in three rounds or less, turn to **248**.

If combat lasts longer than three rounds, turn to **160**.

51

After several attempts, you finally manage to ignite a flame. It flares brightly but soon goes out as it quickly consumes what little oxygen remains in the bubble. Clawing at your throat and chest, you drop slowly to your knees as you suffocate in this transparent, airless tomb.

Your life and your quest end here.

52

Mustering your reserves of psychic strength, you focus your skill at the tumbling trunk. You manage to slow its fall and lock one end into a hollow in the last stair. For a moment it stands upright, wavering from side to side like a gigantic metronome, before falling across the gap with a tremendous crash. When the dust clears, you find yourself staring at a perfect bridge. You waste no time traversing the gap and quickly make your way up the stairs to the breached fortress wall.

Turn to **27**.

53

The pain quickly becomes unbearable (lose 5 ENDURANCE points). As you reel back in agony, the drumming increases speed: unless you act quickly it will destroy your mind.

If you wish to attack the hand, turn to **136**.

If you have a Fireseed and wish to throw it at the plinth, turn to **157**.

If you wish to run between the two green pillars and escape into the passage beyond, turn to **103**.

54

Your basic Kai skills tell you that the lock that secures the door is magical, not mechanical, in nature. All attempts to discover its secret are blocked by the spell that shields the lock. Reluctantly, you abandon the door and leave the chamber by the stairs.

Turn to **193**.

55

At the bottom of the stairs is a deserted hallway that leads to two great doors of gleaming bronze. Sumptuous tapestries and statuettes of gold line the walls on either side, and an ornate fountain of silvered marble fills the hall with a melodious bubbling sound.

You have covered only a few yards when an armoured guard steps into view from behind the fountain. He is armed with a crossbow and is taking aim at your chest.

Pick a number from the *Random Number Table*. If you have the Magnakai Discipline of Huntmastery or

Divination, add 3 to the number you have picked.

If your total is now *0–2*, turn to **189**.
If it is *3* or more, turn to **62**.

56

Swiftly you search the bodies of the slain beastmen, looking for anything that could shed some light on the mysteries of the fortress. After emptying their packs and pockets, you sift through the following Items:

> 2 Axes (Weapons)
> 1 Bow (Weapons)
> 2 Spears (Weapons)
> 1 Quiver with 4 Arrows (Weapons List)
> Enough food for 4 Meals (Meals)
> Pouch of Herbs (Backpack Items)
> Flask of Wine (Backpack Items)

If you have the Magnakai Discipline of Curing and wish to identify the herbs, turn to **129**.

If you wish to examine the sarcophagus, turn to **83**.

If you wish to leave the hall by the tunnel to your left, turn to **201**.

If you prefer to enter the tunnel from which the beastmen appeared, turn to **323**.

57

You sense that neither the rope nor the rocks are quite what they seem: a terrible aura of wickedness hangs over them both. Your try to delve deeper but your concentration is broken when your boat lurches violently towards the jetty. A collision is only seconds away.

If you wish to dive overboard to avoid being
dashed against the stone wall, turn to **325**.

If you wish to grab one of the hanging ropes, turn
to **203**.

If you prefer to close your eyes and pray, turn to
239.

58

You sweep the yawning void but with no success.
Suddenly the footsteps halt. You hear a piercing
crack like that of a whip, and an angry red weal opens
across the back of your hand (lose 2 ENDURANCE
points.) You feel his presence but you cannot see the
enemy who dealt you this wound.

If you wish to continue to search for a crossing, turn
to **44**.

If you wish to stand and fight your unseen enemy,
turn to **257**.

59

The passage becomes hotter and noisier the deeper
you explore it. Unless you have the Magnakai
Discipline of Nexus and have reached the rank of
Primate, you must now deduct 3 ENDURANCE points

from your total due to the suffocating heat and choking, sulphurous fumes. Another tunnel looms out of the yellowish mist to your right. With watery eyes, you peer down it; a red glow fills a crack in the distance. The ground vibrates to an incessant screeching of metallic objects scraping against stone and steel, and this noise, together with the stinking atmosphere, conspires to numb your senses.

If you wish to investigate the red glow, turn to **144**.
If you decide to ignore it and press on along the tunnel, turn to **71**.

60

As soon as your hand touches the mist, a terrific bolt of blue lightning arcs towards it from one corner of the ceiling. Pain shoots up your arm and you are catapulted into the water by the shock (lose 4 ENDURANCE points).

If you have a Vial of Blue Pills, turn to **230**.
If you do not possess this Item, turn to **263**.

61

Your light flares brightly in the moist gloom of the passage. A cavern lies immediately ahead, its high-arched roof a mass of dripping stalactites, hanging like thick spears of pearly white stone. Cautiously, you step across the cavern floor, your skin prickling, as peculiar sounds emanate from the shadows.

You wind your way through the labyrinth of tunnels, slipping on moss-covered rocks, grazing your head on low ceilings and scrambling up and down steep ridges and rockfalls until you arrive at a smooth-walled chamber carved with precision from the hard black rock. A staircase ascends through an archway to your left, and directly ahead stands a massive stone door.

If you wish to examine the stone door, turn to **274**.
If you wish to ascend the stairs, turn to **193**.

62

The guard fires as you run at him, the sneer on his face boasting his confidence that you will soon be a dead man. You twist aside to avoid the lethal bolt, escaping with nothing more serious than a torn sleeve, and shattering his confidence. You attack and he attempts to parry your first blow with his empty crossbow; you knock it from his trembling fingers, leaving him without a weapon to hand.

Throne-hall Guard:
COMBAT SKILL 14   ENDURANCE 22

If you win the combat, turn to **282**.

63 – *Illustration IV*

You crouch in total silence, every nerve and muscle tensed in readiness for combat. A new sound reaches your ears. It does not come from the chamber, but from the tunnel in which you are hiding; it is the sound of a cracking shell.

You turn to see a mass of slimy, twisting serpents, each as long and as thick as your arm, hatching from one of the eggs. Instinctively, they slither towards you, attracted by your body heat and driven on by an insatiable desire for food.

IV. You turn to see a mass of slimy, twisting serpents hatching
from the eggs

If you have the Magnakai Discipline of Invisibility, turn to **281**.

If you have the Magnakai Discipline of Animal Control, turn to **210**.

If you have neither of these skills, turn to **178**.

64

You have walked less than ten feet along the corridor when you are knocked off your feet by a terrible numbing blow to your chest. The ghostly outline of a skeletal warrior shimmers in the air above you, a bloodied spear gripped in its fleshless hands. The wound is fatally deep and the image soon fades into darkness as your life's blood ebbs away.

Your life and your quest end here.

65

You have a strong feeling that the entrance is guarded by a trap. The sickening odour reminds you of your first hunting trip as a Kai initiate to the foothills of the Durncrag mountains of Sommerlund. By chance you discovered an old bear pit that housed a colony of marsh vipers. The awful smell that arose from that pit is identical to the stench seeping from the cave mouth.

If you wish to enter the cave, turn to **258**.

If you decide to return to the beach below, turn to **30**.

66

You study the plate that blocks the locking mechanism. If you could just turn it aside, you might be able to release the lock.

If you have a sword, turn to **252**.

If you do not have a sword, you will have to abandon the door. Only the statue offers any hope of escape for you; turn to **168**.

67

Your arrow sings through the smoky air and pierces the dog-like skull of the leading creature. It halts, as if frozen to the spot, and a sizzling sound emanates from its open jaws. Then, with a flash, it bursts into flames. The fire consumes the creature completely in a matter of seconds and its body disintegrates, dropping to the floor in glowing sticky lumps like molten lava. The other creatures appear undaunted by this and quicken their unnatural gait. With a rasping click, curved talons shoot from their webbed fingers in preparation for attack.

If you wish to fire another arrow, turn to **175**.

If you decide to shoulder your bow and escape into the archway opposite, turn to **241**.

68

The sword itself appears plain and unremarkable but the block on which it rests gives off a strong aura of magic. Your Kai mastery makes you wary of stepping any closer.

If you have the Magnakai Discipline of Nexus, turn to **124**.

If you have a Rope and wish to try to lasso the sword, turn to **182**.

If you decide to ignore the sword and leave the vault by the left tunnel, turn to **298**.

If you prefer to leave by the right tunnel, turn to **322**.

69

The purple-robed creatures rise, shrieking, from their table, their long fingers pointing accusingly at you. In an instant, the corridor beyond is filled with the harsh clang of an alarm bell. Black-clad armoured guards, like those you encountered earlier, appear at the archway, their weapons drawn and their visors closed for combat. They take one look at you and hurl themselves forward in a frenzied attack.

If you have a bow and wish to use it, turn to **50**.
If you decide to defend yourself with a hand weapon, turn to **316**.

70

The Zagothal is totally blind and completely deaf. By using your Kai mastery to mask the scent and heat of your body, you manage to avoid the creature's attack and make your escape towards the distant rock wall. Here, you discover a fissure running vertically through the jet-black stone and are about to enter when the rustle and slither of unseen things echoing in the darkness makes you hesitate.

If you wish to enter the fissure, turn to **16**.
If you prefer to continue your escape along the beach turn to **173**.

71

Half-blinded by the fumes, you fail to see a trip wire strung knee-high across the corridor, but, as soon as you feel it touch your leg, your lightning-fast survival instincts alert you to a trap. There is a rumble in the ceiling and two walls of stone begin to fall simultaneously, threatening to seal off the tunnel on either side.

If you wish to try to dive through the shrinking gap ahead, turn to **337**.

If you decide to dive under the descending wall behind you, turn to **169**.

If you chose to stay where you are, turn to **37**.

72

The creature's flaming fists scorch your tunic but your Kai mastery enables you to survive the worst of the searing heat (lose 2 ENDURANCE points). The attack is wild and haphazard and you have no difficulty avoiding the blows. Ducking beneath the creature's arm, you sprint away towards the jets of flame in the hope of evading the attack, but the sight of the inferno ahead makes you hesitate.

If you wish to enter the flame-jets, turn to **204**.

If you choose to stand and fight the Flame-man, turn to **126**.

73

Taking hold of a crate, you pull open the lid as easily as if you were tearing the peel from an overripe orange. The damp timber crumbles in your hands, falling on the tarnished pewter plates lying within. Your boot staves in the side of another crate, and you hear the dull crunch of shattered porcelain. This one is full of old Kakush vases, part of a cargo from a trading barge that sank on the reef over a decade ago.

You are about to leave when something unusual catches your eye: the tip of a cylindrical map case is jutting out from behind an empty cask. Unlike everything else in this foul room, it is both dry and quite new. Flipping the brass catch, you tip the contents into your palm: a small piece of parchment and a Diamond (you may keep this Special Item in your pocket). A snake with one large eye is drawn in red ink on the parchment. It is coiled around the number **123**. Make a note of this number in the margin of your *Action Chart* – it may be of use to you later in your adventure.

Satisfied that there is nothing else of use or interest in the room, you leave and press on towards the stairs.

Turn to **11**.

74

The tapestries are similar to others you have seen in the lower levels of Kazan-Oud, they are extremely beautiful and exceedingly valuable. However, it is what you discover behind them that is of greater interest, for they conceal a secret door. Your basic Kai senses alert you to a tiny button set into the wall. You press it and the door slides open to reveal a circular tunnel of gleaming steel. Quickly you enter and the door slides shut, moments before the hall is filled with Zahda's guards.

Fifty feet along the gleaming steel tube, you arrive at a circular door in the wall to your left.
If you wish to open the door and enter, turn to **15**.
If you wish to continue along the tube, turn to **90**.

75

Your arrow grazes his shoulder but does not stop him from reaching the rope. In an instant, the harsh clangour of an alarm bell fills the corridor. More armoured guards appear, their weapons drawn and their visors closed for combat. They take one look at their wounded comrade and hurl themselves along the corridor in a frenzied attack. They strike as one and you are forced to engage them as a single enemy.

Zahda Beastmen:
COMBAT SKILL 30   ENDURANCE 39

If you win the combat in three rounds or less, turn to **248**.

If combat lasts longer than three rounds, turn to **160**.

76

The Lekhor twists and writhes in frustrated fury, for it cannot shake you free from its trunk. The head rears up and a droplet of venom splashes the back of your hand. It burns like a red-hot dagger and you cannot stifle a cry of pain. The serpent snickers, its red forked tongue lashing the air just a few inches in front of your face.

Lekhor: COMBAT SKILL 16   ENDURANCE 30

Due to your precarious position, you cannot make use of a shield during the combat, and, due to the corrosive venom of the Lekhor, you must *treble* any ENDURANCE point losses you sustain during the combat.

If you win the combat, turn to **296**.

77

A searing pain explodes behind your eyes as the hand

clamps itself to your head. As the decaying fingers pierce your scalp, forcing their way through your skull, your vision turns red and your body shakes uncontrollably. The hideous claw burrows deeper, feeding on the only source of nourishment than can sustain its existence: living human brain.

Your life and your quest end here.

78 – *Illustration V*

The great wolf slams into your chest, ramming you to the ground with the weight of its massive body. Fangs rake your arm and burning saliva splashes your face. Desperately you stab and slice at its throat, fighting with all the strength and skill you can muster to free yourself from this merciless beast. The creature is immune to Mindblast (but not Psi-surge).

Hound of Death:
COMBAT SKILL 22   ENDURANCE 40

If you win the combat, turn to **341**.

79

Horror twists the warrior's face as your arrow whistles through the air. He opens his mouth to scream but the cry dies in his throat as your shaft buries itself deep in his chest. He staggers, his arms outstretched as if to grab at a rail, and tumbles from the walkway into the smoky chasm.

A hungry shriek resounds from the arch. You draw another arrow and take aim at the darkness as a murmur of low mutterings becomes audible. The sounds chill you. Gurgling and hissing through clenched teeth, three creatures, their skins as black as

V. The Hound of Death slams into your chest, ramming you
    to the ground with the weight of its massive body

night, creep from the shadows and fix you with terrible fiery eyes. They cackle repulsively and slink forward with long loping strides.

If you wish to try to kill all three with your bow, turn to **328**.

If you decide to shoulder your bow and evade them by escaping into the archway opposite, turn to **241**.

80

Despite the alarm bell and the sound of running feet, you make a quick search of the bodies before descending the stairs. Your search uncovers the following Items:

> 1 Spear
> 2 Short Swords
> 1 Axe
> 2 Daggers
> 1 Mace
> 6 Gold Crowns

If you choose to keep any of these Items, remember to make the necessary adjustments to your *Action Chart*.

Turn to **55**.

81

The speed of your attack catches your enemy completely off-guard. He attempts to parry your first blow with his empty crossbow but you knock it from his trembling fingers, leaving him without a weapon to hand.

Throne-hall Guard:
COMBAT SKILL 14   ENDURANCE 22

If you win the combat, turn to **105**.

82

As you mount the slippery stone steps, a roll of distant thunder rumbles across the lake and a few drops of rain spatter the hood of your Kai cloak. A great storm is brewing. By the time you have climbed all the way to the cave mouth, a fierce wind lashes the rock wall and the ground vibrates with every clap of thunder that follows flashes of awful green lightning. Foul air greets your arrival. You are anxious to be out of the storm but the sweet stench of decay that assails your nostrils makes you hesitate at the entrance of the cave.

If you have the Magnakai Discipline of Pathsmanship, turn to **65**.

If you wish to enter the cave, turn to **277**.

If you decide not to enter, you have no other option but to descend the stairs to the beach below; turn to **30**.

83

The sarcophagus is covered with intricate carvings depicting a procession of strange creatures: some are part human, part animal; others are wholly alien to anything you have ever encountered before. One carving in particular holds your attention: that of a snake coiled around a row of three stone buttons. It reminds you of a lock designed by the locksmiths of Holmgard, the capital city of your homeland.

Your keen eyes are drawn to a faint crack that runs vertically through the stone. You follow the line of the crack and discover that it marks the outline of a concealed door.

If you wish to try to open the concealed door, turn
to **115**.

If you prefer to leave the hall by the tunnel to your
right, turn to **323**.

If you wish to leave the hall via the tunnel to your
left, turn to **201**.

84

You meet with no resistance: your hand pushes
through the bubble's skin as if you were dipping it in
water. However, when you try to withdraw it, the
transparent membrane closes around your wrist in a
vice-like grip. As the wolf's jaws snap shut around
your legs the bubble envelopes the upper half of your
body.

In the space of one grisly minute, you are simultaneously suffocated and torn to shreds.

Your life and your quest end here.

85

The climb proves to be one of the most difficult you
have ever attempted. There are precious few places

for you to put your feet and for much of the climb your arms have to support all your weight. Progress is slow and painful, and your efforts are further hampered by gusts of wind and rain.

Pick a number from the *Random Number Table* and add 2. If you possess the Magnakai Discipline of Huntmastery and have reached the Kai rank of Primate you may deduct 2 from this total figure. Your final figure equals the number of ENDURANCE points lost due to wounds and fatigue before you reach the opposite side.

Aching and exhausted, you climb to the top of the stairs and approach the breached fortress wall.

Turn to **27**.

86

You press yourself between two of the silky cocoons hanging from the wall and use your Magnakai skill to mask the heat and scent of your body. The hideous worm-like creature halts, its clicking mandibles snapping the air in frustration. You turn your head away and look straight into one of the cocoons. A chill runs down your spine, for the decaying remains of a female warrior's face stare back at you from inside the web-like strands of the cocoon.

The sudden shock makes you draw breath sharply. Immediately, the worm-like thing slithers forward, propelled by its short, rubbery legs. You can only pray that it has not detected your hiding place.

Pick a number from the *Random Number Table*.

If the number you have picked is *0–4*, turn to **109**.
If it is *5–9*, turn to **278**.

87

'Stick with me,' shouts the warrior over his shoulder as you race along the walkway, the creatures hot on your heels. Events are happening too quickly for you to rationalize your actions; instinct is now your only guide. At the arch he suddenly stops, throwing his arms out wide to hold you back. You run headlong into him with a jolt that leaves you breathless, but his strong hands grab your Backpack and keep you on your feet.

'Snake-trap!' he shouts, pointing to a stone slab set into the floor. 'Curse this infernal place; is nowhere safe from Zahda's devilry?' A shriek of malicious glee makes you turn your head; the creatures are closer than you feared. 'Jump!' cries the warrior. 'For pity's sake, jump!'

If you wish to jump across the slab, turn to **268**.

If you decide to stand and fight the onrushing enemy, turn to **299**.

88

Jets of fire spurt from the floor and walls momentarily blinding you. A wave of searing heat buffets your face, singeing your hair and eyelashes (lose 2 ENDURANCE points), and forcing you to retreat for fear of being burned alive.

Suddenly there is a ghastly scream. Something is approaching you through the flames. In the next instant, a blazing human form staggers into view; it shrieks in agony and lurches out of the fire-jets, its arms flailing wildly as it launches an attack.

If you wish to prepare to defend yourself, turn to **126**.

If you wish to run past the fiery attacker and into the blazing inferno, turn to **204**.

If you wish to evade both by running back along the tunnel, turn to **320**.

If you have the Magnakai Discipline of Nexus, turn to **72**.

89

You sense that the bridge is strong enough to support your weight, so long as it is not subjectd to any sudden or violent shock. Such a shock could easily open up one of the many cracks that riddle its core.

Forewarned by your Kai mastery, you step on to the bridge and advance carefully.

Turn to **243**.

90

As you walk the temperature steadily rises until you are bathed in sweat. The steel plates of the tunnel become too hot to touch and wisps of smoke rise from the soles of your boots, where the leather is close to igniting.

If you have that Magnakai Discipline of Nexus, or a Platinum Amulet, turn to **24**.

If you have neither the skill or the Special Item, turn to **324**.

91

To your dismay, you discover that the tunnel is no more than a shallow cave that shelters a clutch of eggs, each one as large as a barrel of ale. They lie upon a bed of packs and torn clothing, all that remains of previous adventurers who fell foul of the giant snake. An angry snickering and a stabbing forked tongue force you to the back of the tunnel, warning you that a similar fate may lie in store for you.

If you wish to examine the eggs more closely, turn to **148**.

If you wish to search for a way to escape from the tunnel, turn to **346**.

92

You advance along the passage, confident of your ability to deal with the sudden appearance of any guard who should be unfortunate enough to cross your path. Dark openings loom on either side and you scrutinize the floor ahead for any signs of a trap or pit.

The passage becomes dank and dark. Whip cracks, screams and sounds of weeping echo in the distance: the pitiful sounds of torture.

If you wish to continue along the passage, turn to **36**.

If you wish to retrace your steps and take the other passage, turn to **20**.

93

Cleaving a path through the thick cobwebs proves more difficult that you anticipated. Sticky rope-like strands soon cover you from head to foot and, to your horror, they begin to shrink. It is too late to evade this attack – you must fight for your life. The enemy is immune to Mindblast and Psi-surge. Owing to your restricted ability to move, reduce your

COMBAT SKILL by 4 points for the duration of the combat.

Trap-webs: COMBAT SKILL 14   ENDURANCE 34

If you win the fight, turn to **131**.

94

You glance back over your shoulder just as the wolf reaches the corner. The sight of its gleaming fangs makes your skin crawl with fear, but, to your surprise, it does not continue the chase. It stops and rests on its haunches, its horrible face lined with fear and frustration as it watches you disappear into the gloom.

Turn to **240**.

95

The warrior is halfway across the walkway when a hungry shriek resounds from the arch. He spins on his heel and crouches in readiness for combat. A murmur of low mutterings follows; the sound chills you. Then gurgling and hissing through clenched teeth, three creatures, their shiny skins as black as night, creep from the shadows and fix you both with fiery stares. The warrior beings to shake, his sword wavering in his gloved hand. As the creatures stalk forward, his nerve breaks and he turns and flees towards you.

'Save yourself, stranger. They'll eat you alive!'

If you wish to run with the warrior and evade the creatures by escaping into the archway opposite, turn to **87**.

If you wish to attack the warrior as soon as he is close, turn to **345**.

If you decide to let him pass and face the creatures alone, turn to **249**.

96

As the blade leaves the block there is a tremendous howl, like that of a mountain wolf baying at a full moon. Your heart leaps into your mouth and you back away hurriedly, half-expecting it to change into a ravening monster at any second. It takes several minutes for your fears to subside.

Cursing your predicament, you sheathe your new-found weapon and ponder which exit to take from the vault.

If you wish to take the left tunnel, turn to **48**.
If you wish to take the right tunnel, turn to **176**.

97

The creature seems immune to your attack. Swiftly the tendril writhes past you, coiling itself twice before tightening around your neck. With a merciless jolt, it wrenches you away from the fissure and drags you towards its ghastly mouth.

Terror and pain give way to blind desperation as its fetid breath washes over your trembling face.

If you have any Fireseeds, turn to **10**.
If you possess the Sommerswerd, turn to **317**.
If you have neither of these Special Items, turn to **331**.

98

Cautiously you walk around the throne, your weapon held out in readiness to strike. As you draw level, your heart leaps into your mouth – you are staring into the cold, unblinking eyes of Lord Zahda. He sneers evilly and points a rod of inlaid platinum at your head.

If you possess the Sommerswerd, turn to **174**.
If you do not have this Special Item, turn to **202**.

99

You sense that the air in the north tunnel is far hotter than that of the west. Judging by the smell of sulphur that pervades the cavern you guess that some form of volcanic activity is taking place to the north.

If you wish to investigate this activity, turn to **59**.
If you decide that the west tunnel would be safer, turn to **323**.

100 – *Illustration VI (overleaf)*

You enter a chamber where a tall bronze statue stands. You recognize its distinctive head-dress and robes immediately: it is a Zakhan, a ruler of the desert empire of Vassagonia. The statue looks most distressed: its arms are outstretched in a gesture of hopelessness, and the expression on its face is one of sorrow and despair. Beyond the statue, an oval-shaped door is set flush in the wall but you discover that it is locked.

The mist grows brighter. Once more the skull appears and speaks, its voice as comforting as a raven's croak:

> 'Listen to the Zakhan,
> Ponder what you hear;
> Give the correct answer,
> For fear he sheds a tear.'

VI.   You enter a chamber where a tall bronze statue stands: it is
Zakhan, ruler of Vassagonia

The skull disappears into the misty ceiling and you watch amazed as the dull bronze lips of the statue begin to move. A harsh voice echoes from deep within its hollow metal body:

'My daughter has many sisters, as many sisters as she has brothers, but each of her brothers has twice as many sisters as brothers. So answer me this, wise warrior, how many sons and daughters do I have?'

Consider your answer carefully and, when you have decided, write down first the number of sons the Zakhan has, and then, immediately next to it, the number of daughters. Now turn to the entry which bears the same number as your answer.

If you cannot answer the Zakhan's riddle, turn to **270**.

101

Without any warning, a solid iron door slams down behind your back, sealing off the entrance to the chamber. The distant sound of rattling chains and sliding bolts makes your pulse quicken, and instinctively you reach for your weapon to defend yourself against a sudden attack. Several uneventful minutes pass before you relax your guard.

If you decide to find out where the tunnel leads, turn to **277**.

If you wish to try to force open the iron door, turn to **214**.

102

The panel slides shut of its own accord and the buttons click back to their original positions.

If you wish to leave the hall by the tunnel to your left, turn to **201**.

If you decide to leave by the tunnel to your right, the same tunnel by which the black-clad warriors entered the hall, turn to **323**.

103

You run straight into an invisible barrier, a field of destructive energy that flows between the two green pillars. With a thunderous concussion, you are repelled from the shield and sent tumbling back into the chamber (lose 8 ENDURANCE points; lose only 6 ENDURANCE points if you have the Magnakai Discipline of Nexus).

If you are still alive, turn to **116**.

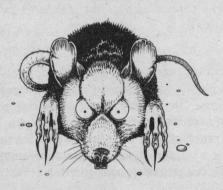

104

Unless you possess the Magnakai Discipline of Nexus, by the time you reach the fissure you have lost 3 ENDURANCE points due to the effect of the scorching sand. Standing at the jagged opening, you hear the rustle and slither of unseen things echoing within the depths of the darkness. Suddenly something round and black breaks through the surface of the lake. A hideous gurgling cry splits the night as the thing hurtles across the beach towards you.

> If you wish to take cover inside the fissure, turn to **16**.
> If you wish to draw a weapon and prepare for combat, turn to **342**.
> If you have a bow and wish to use it, turn to **225**.

105

You race over to your companion's side and discover that he is still conscious, although he has lost a lot of blood. Using your healing skill, you repair the wound as best you can, but it is deep and severe and you can only prolong his life for a few minutes at most. You tell him of your quest and the help the Elder Magi have given to enable you to enter Kazan-Oud. As you recount your air voyage to Herdos aboard Lord Paido's skyship, you notice his eyes flicker in recognition of the name.

'My name is Kasin,' he says, painfully. 'Lord Paido is my brother.' You notice the resemblance in his cat-like eyes and square jaw. 'I'm finished, Kai Lord,' he says, his face bathed in sweat, 'but I can and will help you in your quest. Listen carefully. Over there, behind the tapestry, is a secret passage. It leads to Zahda's throne. Above the throne is the Lorestone of Herdos, but beware, Zahda has coupled its power to a Doomstone from the realm of Naaros. He draws his power from that accursed gem. If you are to succeed, you must first destroy the Doomstone or you will surely perish. Sadly, I cannot help you escape from Kazan-Oud, for I myself was captured long before I reached the surface, but if you can get to the beach, make your way to the old stone jetty. I hid my boat beneath the steps there.' His grip tightens around your hand as a wave of pain washes over his body. 'When you return to Elzian, he gasps, 'tell my brother that my death was not in vain . . . May the gods protect you . . . Lone Wolf.'

As his eyes close for the last time, you promise that his bravery will live forever in the hearts of the Vakeros – his brave warrior kin.

Turn to **282**.

106

You are less than twenty yards from the west tunnel when an agonizing pain tears through your back and explodes from your chest in a gout of blood and flame. You stagger and fall, your body virtually torn in two by a powerful bolt of destructive energy, and you die within seconds of hitting the hard stone floor.

Slain by a Dhax power-staff, your life and your quest end here.

107

Your hand passes through the surface of the first bubble meeting little resistance; it is as if you are dipping your hand into a pool of water. But when you try to remove it, the rubbery skin closes in a vice-like grip. You fight to free your hand but you only cause the bubble to work its way further up your arm. Soon it envelopes your whole body, locking you within its air-tight skin.

Your eyes bulge and your lungs burn viciously as you fight for air in this transparent prison (lose 6 ENDURANCE points).

If you have a sword and want to try to cut your way out of the bubble, turn to **26**.

If you have a Torch and Tinderbox, or a Lantern, and want to try to burn your way free, turn to **51**.

If you have a Kalte Firesphere, turn to **145**.

If you have none of the above Items, turn to **292**.

108

The swift undercurrent of the stream is so powerful that you are swept along the gully and far out into the lake. The weight of your equipment, your fatigue, and the highly polluted stream water all conspire to sap your strength. You cannot keep your head above the water and lose 5 ENDURANCE points due to lack of oxygen.

Turn to **158**.

109

You fight back your rising nausea as the worm slithers past, its slimy body wiping itself against your back. As soon as it has passed, you leave your hiding place and hurry along the corridor, anxious to put as much distance as possible between the horrible worm and yourself in case it should turn and pursue you.

Turn to **46**.

110 – *Illustration VII (overleaf)*

Four warriors, dark and grim, march into the hall in single file. At once their black armour and skull-like helmets make you think they are Drakkarim – evil human warriors who serve the Darklords of Helgedad. But when they draw to a halt before the sarcophagus, you see that they cannot possibly be human. Their great sloping shoulders support unnaturally long

111

arms, and the hands that grip their weapons are covered with bristling ginger hair. Yellowed talons curve from their fingers, and behind them hang long black tails, tufted at the end like the tails of lions.

Their leader grunts a command and approaches the grey granite tomb. He raises his hairy fist and presses three buttons set into the stone. A secret panel slides open and all four step into it and disappear from view. It closes behind them without a sound.

If you wish to examine the sarcophagus, turn to **83**.
If you wish to leave the hall by the tunnel from which the warriors appeared, turn to **323**.
If you decide to leave the hall by the tunnel to your left, turn to **201**.

111

You are standing in a passage, the walls and floor of which are completely sheer and smooth. Overhead swirls a mist that gives off a dim diffused light, just sufficient for you to be able to see your way ahead. Without your weapons you feel naked and vulnerable, but you take some comfort in the fact that you still have your Backpack, your Gold Crowns and your Special Items.

Cautiously you walk along the passage, expecting the unexpected, until you arrive at a circular vault. There, upon a block of marble in the centre of the floor, lies a steel sword. As you step into the vault, slabs of stone sink into the floor to reveal two exits: one to your left, the other to your right.

If you have the Magnakai Discipline of Divination or Psi-screen, turn to **68**.

VII.   Four warriors, dark and grim, march into the hall – they
cannot possibly be human

If you wish to pick up the sword, turn to **224**.

If you wish to enter the left tunnel, turn to **298**.

If you wish to enter the right tunnel, turn to **322**.

112

The arrow pierces the centre of the sphere and disappears completely. Fearing that your missile has proved harmless, you shoulder your bow and are about to draw a hand weapon when suddenly there is a flash of light and a tremendous explosion. The black sphere bursts into thousands of pieces, and is consumed in a fireball of brilliant yellow flame. A wave of heat sears your face (lose 1 ENDURANCE point) and you are hurled backwards into the fissure by the blast.

Turn to **16**.

113

The creaking door stirs the man from sleep and he rolls over and cowers in the corner of his foul-smelling cage. His eyes are cloudy, like frosted glass, and his face and hands are pitted with disease.

If you have the Magnakai Discipline of Curing, turn to **192**.

If you do not have this skill, turn to **247**.

114

Your efforts have jammed up the door, creating enough space for you to squeeze underneath. You crawl into the chamber beyond and, aching with fatigue, stagger to your feet. You pause to catch your breath before entering the northern tunnel.

Turn to **187**.

115

If the lock operates in the same way as those made by the Locksmith's Guild of Holmgard, you need only press each button once to open the door. But in which order should you press them?

If you wish to press the first, then second, then third button, turn to **123**.

If you wish to press the second, then third, then first button, turn to **231**.

If you wish to press the second, then first, then third button, turn to **213**.

If you wish to press the third, then first, then second button, turn to **312**.

If you wish to press the third, then second, then first button, turn to **321**.

If you wish to press the first, then third, then second button, turn to **132**.

116

To your horrified amazement, the hand springs into the air and hovers above your head. Writhing fingers stretch open as the hand plummets towards your skull.

Pick a number from the *Random Number Table*. If you have the Magnakai Discipline of Huntmastery, add 3 to the number you have picked.

If your total is now *0–2*, turn to **77**.

If it is *3–6*, turn to **198**.

If it is 7 or more, turn to **235**.

117

The rats are unafraid of the water. They hurl themselves at you, clawing and biting at your back as

118

you push the coracle out into the icy cold lake. Tumbling into the little boat, you swiftly despatch the most determined of the rodents before paddling away from the bay. You have covered barely a hundred yards when the coracle lists heavily to one side. The rats have chewed through the wood below the waterline and you are sinking fast.

If you have the Magnakai Discipline of Curing, turn to **234**.

If you do not possess this skill, or do not wish to use it, turn to **325**.

118

A wave of energy surges through your body as you close your hand around the Lorestone of Herdos (restore your ENDURANCE points score to its original total). Your senses tingle and a new-found strength wipes away the fatigue of your terrible ordeal, enabling you to assess the situation anew. You step into the blue beam and immediately you are drawn upwards, following closely on the heels of Zahda, who is struggling to stay in the centre of the column of light. He is gripped with mortal fear of you and, as he sees you gaining on him, he unsheathes a glowing dagger and inverts himself to face you as you approach. When you are at arm's length he launches a wild attack. Lord Zahda is immune to Mindblast (but not Psi-surge). If you have the Magnakai Discipline of Huntmastery, add 2 to your COMBAT SKILL for the duration of the fight.

Lord Zahda: COMBAT SKILL 23   ENDURANCE 45

If you win the combat, turn to **200**.

119

Your basic Kai skill of tracking enables you to stay on Tavig's trail. As you retrace the route you took earlier, your mind is filled with urgent questions. Who or what is the Trakka? Where do the Dhax come from? Who is Zahda that Tavig spoke of so fearfully?

Suddenly your thoughts are shattered by a scream that resounds from the top of a staircase directly ahead. Tavig appears, clutching his face, blood trickling through his fingers. He is about to fall when the scaly green fingers of a gigantic hand reach out of the darkness and snatch him back. He vanishes from sight but his screams grow louder.

If you wish to charge up the stairs to try to save him, turn to **280**.

If you wish to escape in the opposite direction, turn to **323**.

120

The wolf leaps at your chest, its claws ripping your tunic as it slams you to the ground with its monstrous weight (lose 4 ENDURANCE points). Fangs flash before your eyes and fetid saliva splashes your face as you fight desperately to save yourself from the jaws of death.

Suddenly there is a ghastly scream. The wolf pulls away, its eyes fixed fearfully on the roaring jets of flame. At that moment a human form staggers into view, shrieking in agony and lurching from side to side; the wolf howls and lopes away as the flaming apparition stumbles forward, its arms flailing as it launches a wild atttack.

If you wish to defend yourself, turn to **126**.

If you wish to run past the fiery attacker and into the roaring jets of flame, turn to **204**.

If you have the Magnakai Discipline of Nexus, turn to **72**.

121

The tentacle lifts you into the air, tightening its grip with each passing second until almost all the breath is squeezed from your lungs. Suddenly you are hurled towards another massive boulder, which opens to reveal a monstrous jaw dripping with loathsome saliva. You are swallowed whole.

Your life and your quest end here.

122

You are forced to cut a path through the horde of creatures that huddle on the steps leading to the jetty. Creatures are crawling out of the ground itself: every-where you look black slimy hands are bursting through the surface, squeezing their way free from Kazan-Oud through the scores of fissures opening up in the sheer rock wall.

Near to the base of the steps, you are dragged to the ground by a clutch of loathsome slaves. They pay dearly for their mistake but not before your Backpack is torn from your shoulders (erase your Backpack and all that it contained from your *Action Chart*).

When you reach the jetty you are covered from head to toe in the blood of your foes. The sight is so frightening that all resistance melts away and creatures hurl themselves into the lake rather than face the fearsome straight-backed, white-skinned killer of their kin. Beneath the jetty steps you discover an arch, sealed off at one end and with a weed-encrusted stone door at the other. Inside is a small wicker coracle and a paddle.

Having fought off the most determined of Kazan-Oud's horrors, you launch the coracle, jump aboard and paddle frantically towards the distant glimmer of the power-shield. The deafening death-cry of Kazan-Oud echoes in your ears.

Turn to **350**.

123

As you press the third button you hear a distinct click. The panel slides open and you find yourself staring down a flight of steps that lead to a strong iron-shod door.

If you wish to enter the sarcophagus, turn to **216**.
If you choose not to enter, turn to **102**.

124

By focusing your Kai skill on the sword, you can cause it to rise from the marble block and move through the air towards you.

If you wish to use your mastery of Nexus in this
way, turn to **279**.

If you decide to leave the sword undisturbed and
leave the vault by the left tunnel, turn to **298**.

If you decide to leave by the right tunnel, turn to **322**.

125

His heart beats a dozen times then stops. You close
his sightless eyes and lay his sword upon his chest, in
the custom of the land of Slovia when a warrior falls in
battle.

If you decide to leave the body and continue, turn
to **323**.

If you wish to search the body before you go, turn
to **227**.

126

With a cry that shakes your soul, the creature leaps
forward to claw at your throat. The creature is
immune to Mindblast (but not Psi-surge). Unless you
have the Magnakai Discipline of Nexus, double all
ENDURANCE points that you lose during the combat,
due to the severity of the burns you sustain.

Flame-man: COMBAT SKILL 14   ENDURANCE 40

If you win the combat, turn to **147**.

127

You clear the slab with one bound and press on along
the winding tunnel. A warm, damp wind, whistles
along the rough-walled passage, carrying with it a
rancid smell of sulphur and decay. For over an hour
you walk down the tunnel, leaping over fissures in the

uneven floor and taking care not to tread on glistening blue-black worms that slither away into cracks in the rock when your light invades their damp, dark world.

Eventually the tunnel opens out into an oval-shaped chamber. A staircase, festooned with cobwebs, ascends to an open trap door in the ceiling. The familiar pale green glow of the power-shield filters in through this portal. At the foot of the stairs lies the mouldering remains of a body partially encased in armour. A rusty sword is clenched in its skeletal fist, and a bone-handled dagger protrudes from the base of its skull.

If you wish to climb the stairs to the open trap door, turn to **93**.

If you wish to examine the remains of the body more closely, turn to **199**.

If you wish to leave the chamber and continue along the tunnel, turn to **318**.

128

As the flames die down and the smoke clears, you see the blackened hand lying at the base of the plinth. To your horror and amazement it begins to move, flexing its charred fingers jerkily. Open-mouthed, you stare in disbelief as it suddenly springs into the air and hovers above your head. Its writhing fingers stretch open as it plummets towards your skull.

Pick a number from the *Random Number Table*. If you have the Magnakai Discipline of Huntmastery, add 3 to the number you have picked.

If your total is now *0–1*, turn to **77**.

(continued over)

If it is *2–6*, turn to **198**.
If it is 7 or more, turn to **235**.

129

You recognize the herbs to be crushed Adgana leaves, a plant that grows in abundance in the Bavari Hills of northern Dessi. One dose is enough to increase your COMBAT SKILL by 6 points for the duration of a fight.

However, Adgana is shunned by most professional warriors and its use is outlawed in the Lastlands because it is highly addictive. If you decide to take this potion prior to combat, there is a small chance that you could become addicted. As soon as the combat is resolved, you must pick a number from the *Random Number Table*. If the number you pick is *0* or *1*, you have become addicted and your ENDURANCE score must be reduced by 4 points. This reduction is a permanent loss to your basic ENDURANCE points score.

Should the opportunity to use a further dose of Adgana ever arise, its effect on that occasion will be only half that of the original dose (ie, it will increase your COMBAT SKILL by 3 points instead of 6).

If you now wish to examine the sarcophagus, turn to **83**.
If you wish to enter the tunnel from which the Beastmen appeared, turn to **323**.
If you wish to leave the hall by the other tunnel, turn to **201**.

130

You stare into the inky black eyes and command the

creature to cease its attack. Instantly the slimy worm-like thing rears up, its short, rubbery legs scrabbling the air in agony, as your command burns into its sensitive and vulnerable brain. As it twists back on itself, its head disappears into the mist. There is an ear-splitting crack as blue lightning engulfs the creature, crackling snake-like around its neck, and filling your nostrils with the stench of burning meat. The creature thrashes wildly for several minutes and, when its gruesome dance is finally done, the canopy of mist is no longer there. In the darkness above, you see a walkway with an observation platform.

If you wish to climb the body of the dead worm-thing and pull yourself on to the platform, turn to **294**.

If you prefer to climb over the worm and continue along the corridor, turn to **46**.

131

Cutting yourself free from the last of the deadly strands, you race headlong up the stairs and out through the open portal. You discover that during the struggle you lost a weapon and one Item from your Backpack (erase a weapon of your choice, and the second item on your list of Backpack Items).

You find yourself standing in the ruins of a small storehouse. Through the shattered pane of glass of the solitary arched window, you can see the eerie outline of broken battlements and a fire-blackened tower. You are staring at the remains of Kazan-Oud.

Turn to **27**.

132

The buttons remain depressed but nothing seems to happen. You are about to abandon your attempt at entry when there is a distinct click. The panel slides open to reveal a set of steps that descends to a large wooden door, reinforced with studs and strips of iron.

If you choose to enter the sarcophagus, turn to **37**.
If you decide not to enter, turn to **102**.

133

Desperately you use your mastery of healing to save his life, applying your power to the open wounds that disfigure his face and throat. The bleeding stops and his heartbeat grows stronger, but you sense that it is only a temporary reprieve. His back is broken and, here, in this hostile fortress, there is no hope for his survival and recovery with so serious an injury. Briefly he regains consciousness and forces himself to speak. 'Beware the maze, northlander . . . green . . . is death.'

It is all he says before slipping away into endless sleep. You close his sightless eyes and lay his sword upon his chest, as is the custom in the land of Slovia when a valiant warrior falls in battle.

If you now decide to leave the body and continue, turn to **323**.

If you wish to search the body before you go, turn to **227**.

134

You feed off the power directed against you, charging your Psi-surge with the energy waves that buffet your psychic shield. With an immense effort of will, you launch pulses of energy at the hand. The vibrations gather power from the hand itself, setting up an explosive reaction that cannot be reversed. Suddenly there is a searing white flash as the hand disintegrates into thousands of tiny fragments. Your head swims with the fatigue of psychic combat (lose 4 ENDURANCE points), but you feel elated by your bloodless victory.

Turn to **334**.

135

A streak of green forked lightning lights up the collapsed roof of Kazan-Oud and, for a second, it looks like the shattered ribs of a giant lizard. There is another flash of lightning and a hundred tower windows glare at you like empty eyes edged with slivers of broken glass. A line of carved stone gargoyles adorns the black stone walls, overhanging the jetty. Rings of rusted iron are clamped in their snarling jaws, each wound round with slime-encrusted ropes that dangle in the water. At the jetty, it is deep enough to allow a large vessel to dock but the current and the swell of the tide make it increasingly difficult for you to control your tiny boat.

Your stomach tightens as the swell threatens to dash you against the jetty.

If you wish to stop paddling and try to grab one of the ropes, turn to **203**.

If you decide to abandon the boat and swim towards a line of rocks further west, turn to **325**.

If you have the Magnakai Discipline of Divination, turn to **57**.

136

As soon as you strike the hand, the psychic attack ceases. Although your blow causes no visible wound, the hand suddenly falls limp and drops to the ground near to the base of the plinth.

If you wish to attack it again, turn to **116**.

If you decide to leave it and pass through the two green pillars and into the passage beyond, turn to **103**.

137

With all your will, you command the snake to come no closer. Its great eye burns you with an icy stare, the black slit pupil shrinking and dilating with every beat of its evil heart. It sways above you, hesitating to attack, as your Kai mastery plants seeds of doubt in its mind, blocking its primeval desire to savage and consume your warm-blooded being. As the monstrous head sways from side to side, you catch a glimpse of a small tunnel in the opposite wall, previously hidden by the snake and its nest. The sight of this possible means of escape momentarily breaks your concentration: the snake lunges forward to attack. Only the speed of your reactions saves you from its venomous fangs. Reluctantly, it retreats at your command and settles in the centre of the chamber, its head resting on its coils as it settles down to sleep.

If you wish to attack the snake, turn to **219**.
If you decide to skirt around it and enter the tunnel,
   turn to **260**.

You unsheathe your weapon and strike a mighty blow
at the black crystal. It splits clean in two, releasing its
dark power and showering you with hot sparks in the
wake of its destruction. The riven fragments hurtle into
the fiery abyss that surrounds Zahda's throne, quash-
ing the roaring flames.

'Curse you, Kai Lord' screams Lord Zahda, leaping
out from behind the golden throne, brandishing a
platinum rod. Defiantly, he points the rod at your head
and spits an evocation, but the power he calls upon no
longer heeds his cry. From the depths of the pit, a
terrible roar begins to grow. the floor shakes and a
column of flame lights the entire throne-hall as molten
lava spews high into the air. Zahda staggers back, his
face aghast with terror. Hurriedly he kneels before his
throne, his crooked fingers stroking at a pentagram
engraved in the gold. Above the din of destruction,
another sound, like the ringing of a thousand tiny bells,
can be heard and in the blackness above the throne a
speckled glow appears. It descends towards Lord
Zahda until he is totally engulfed by a column of
shimmering blue light. His body rises, lifted by unseen
hands.

If you wish to grab the Lorestone and step into the
   column of shimmering blue light, turn to **118**.
If you wish to grab the Lorestone and escape back
   into the steel tube, turn to **250**.

139

Covering the floor of the north tunnel are myriad tiny animal tracks. Rats, mice, worms and snakes, denizens common to every subterranean lair, have all left their mark upon the grime-encrusted flagstones. But the east tunnel bears no such markings. There the ground is smooth and undisturbed, not even a film of dust discolours the grey stone floor. Your senses warn you that this tunnel is more than it seems.

If you now wish to enter the east tunnel, turn to **101**.
If you decide to take the north tunnel, turn to **187**.

140

Your senses heightened by the threat of a gruesome death, you are quick to notice a beam of light crossing the passage ahead at knee height.

If you wish to jump over the beam, turn to **155**.
If you choose to run through the beam, turn to **94**.

141

Wiping away the sweat of battle on your grimy sleeve, you turn to go but, as you do so, you stumble over something lying on the blood-spattered path. At first glance it looks like a mace but closer inspection reveals a slim, silver rod with an orange ball of glass held in a claw at one end. It is far too delicate to be used as a weapon in the normal way.

If you wish to pick up the Silver Sceptre, turn to **223**.
If you wish to leave it where it is and continue, turn to **308**.
If you have completed the Lore-circle of the Spirit, turn to **25**.

142 – *Illustration VIII (overleaf)*

At the end of the cell block corridor a staircase descends to a lower level. It is guarded by a grim-faced creature armed with an axe.

Beastman Gaoler: COMBAT SKILL 17   ENDURANCE 22

If you win the fight in three rounds or less, turn to **238**.

If the fight lasts more than three rounds, turn to **212**.

143

Swiftly the tendril writhes past you, coiling twice before tightening around your neck. With an electrifying jolt, it wrenches you away from the fissure and drags you slowly towards its ghastly mouth.

Terror and pain give way to blind desperation as its fetid breath washes over your trembling face.

If you have any Fireseeds, turn to **10**.

If you possess the Sommerswerd, turn to **317**.

If you have neither of these Special Items, turn to **331**.

144

You inch your way along the tunnel until you reach a dead end. The red glow you saw earlier is pouring through a narrow portal, shaped like a large arrow slit. You look through it at an awesome sight. A cavernous crater, formed of black iron, drops in tiers to a blood-red floor far below. Hundreds of moving forms crowd every level, dragging wagons and pulling monstrous machines up long ramps and across connecting causeways. Other forms dressed in black,

VIII.   The Beastman Gaoler, a grim-faced creature armed with
an axe, guards the staircase

beat and curse them; the heat and fumes that are wafting through the portal prevent you from seeing them more clearly.

Suddenly a solid sheet of iron descends from the ceiling and seals off the portal. You step back and turn to leave, but in the smoky distance you see another wall of iron closing off the exit.

Turn to **37**.

Breaking open the two halves of your Firesphere, you hold the magical flame close to the transparent skin. It quickly melts a hole and a great gust of air surges into the bubble, splitting the skin wide open from top to bottom. Holding the Firesphere before you, you melt a path through the other bubbles. As the flame punctures their jelly-like skins they implode and plop to the floor in tatters.

You move on, your eyes peeled for the slightest hint of danger. A shadow on the floor in the distance makes you wary, and your fear soon turns to dismay when you see that it is a deep, dark pit, which covers the corridor with thirty feet of blackness. A sudden glow in the mist overhead heralds the unwelcome return of the skull:

> 'The path across defies your sight;
> Find the path or stay and fight!'

If you have the Magnakai Discipline of Psi-screen or Divination, turn to **39**.

If you do not possess either of these skills, turn to **261**.

146

The first thing that you notice is the warrior's lack of wounds: no sword cuts or arrow shafts pierce his armour. If it were not for the unmistakable smell of death, you could be forgiven for thinking that he was asleep. You turn the body over to take a look at his face, and recoil in shock at the sight before you. The eyes are missing, leaving two ghastly black holes; the tongue hangs out, dark and swollen, and from the corners of the twisted mouth oozes a thick, greenish fluid. Filled with revulsion, you leave the body and step into the secret passage.

Turn to **11**.

147

A heap of molten ash is now all that remains of the Flame-man. Then, as suddenly as they began, the jets of flame shut off, leaving the passage ahead shimmering with a heat haze. A laugh, cold and distant, echoes above the ceiling of mist, stirring you to curse Lord Zahda and his deadly maze.

Turn to **240**.

148

The eggs are warm and you can feel tiny movements through the leathery shells. Carefully you roll them aside and sift through the debris of the nest; you discover several Items of interest:

MACE (Weapons)
PADDED LEATHER WAISTCOAT (Special Items) Adds
    2 points to your ENDURANCE total when worn.
SWORD (Weapons)

HELMET (Special Items) Adds 2 points to your
 ENDURANCE total when worn
BLANKET (Backpack Items)
BOTTLE OF WINE (Backpack Items)
DAGGER (Weapons)
POTION OF LAUMSPUR (Backpack Items) Restores 4
 ENDURANCE points when swallowed; enough for
 one dose.

If you take any of these Items, remember to adjust
your *Action Chart* accordingly.

The sound of a drawbolt and the creak of a dry hinge
echoes from the chamber behind you, causing your
pulse to race anew. Pick a number from the *Random
Number Table*.

If the number you have picked is *0–4*, turn to **63**.
If it is *5–9*, turn to **346**.

149

Lord Zahda shrieks an unearthly howl as your killing
blow rips open his black heart. He thrusts a pleading,
claw-like hand towards the roof and drops heavily to
his knees, his dying curse lost as blood fills his throat.
His left eye gleams brightly for a second then
suddenly dies, like a candle flaring in a storm before it
is extinguished by the rain. He sways and falls from
the pinnacle to be devoured by the hungry flames of
the pit.

Hurrying over to the throne, you draw back your
weapon and strike the black crystal with a mighty
blow. It splits clean in two, releasing its dark power
and showering you with hot sparks in the wake of its
destruction. The riven fragments hurtle into the fiery

abyss and the flames grow deadly quiet.

From the depths of the pit, a terrible roar begins to grow. The pinnacle shakes and a column of flame lights the entire throne-hall as molten lava spews high into the air.

> If you wish to take the Lorestone and escape into the steel tube, turn to **250**.
> If you wish to take the Lorestone and search for some other way of escape from the throne-hall, turn to **267**.

150

To begin with the shattered steps and hollows pose no problems that your agility and skill cannot overcome. However, as you are nearing the top of the stairs, you suddenly find yourself staring into a yawning void: the steps have been sheared away, leaving a gap over twenty feet side.

> If you have the Magnakai Discipline of Nexus, and wish to use it, turn to **255**.
> If you have a Rope, turn to **310**.
> If you have neither mastery of Nexus nor a Rope, turn to **211**.

151

You cleave a path through the bubbles as easily as if you were scything cobwebs. As your sword punctures their jelly-like skins they implode and plop to the floor in tatters.

You move on, your eyes peeled for the slightest hint of danger. A shadow on the floor in the distance makes you wary. Your fear soon turns to dismay, for, as you grow closer, you can see that it is a deep, dark pit that stretches across the entire corridor. There appears to be no way across. Staring at the opposite side, over thirty feet away, you ponder the impossible task confronting you. A sudden glow in the misty ceiling heralds the return of the skull.

> The path across defies your sight;
> Find the path or stay and fight.'

If you have the Magnakai Discipline of Psi-screen or Divination, turn to **39**.

If you do not possess either of these skills, turn to **261**.

152

Your arrow strikes home, sinking into the side of another creature. The creature jerks backwards and freezes in a ghastly contortion of pain. The thrashing legs of its wounded companion knock it from the walkway and it topples stiffly into the chasm.

Only one creature remains uninjured. It turns on you, its grisly mouth stained green with the blood of its companion.

If you wish to fire another arrow at this enemy, turn to **253**.

If you wish to turn and flee into the archway opposite, turn to **277**.

153

The rising water lifts you, floating you nearer to the swirling mist that is the ceiling of the chamber.

If you wish to try to escape through the mist, turn to **60**.

If you wish to dive down and examine the statue, turn to **168**.

If you have the Magnakai Discipline of Divination, turn to **307**.

154

Flattening yourself against the wall, you watch with growing fear as the trunk crosses the gap and smashes into the steps close to where you stand. A ragged branch cuts open your cheek and another scrapes your ribs, causing you to cry out at the sudden pain (lose 3 ENDURANCE points).

As the tree hits the beach below, it quivers in the black sand like a huge javelin. You wipe away the blood from your face and look once more at the shattered staircase above.

If you have a Rope, turn to **310**.

If you do not possess a Rope, turn to **211**.

155

A flash of intense white light blinds you momentarily as jets of fire spurt from the floor and walls. They are so bright and numerous that you cannot see where they end. A searing wave of heat scorches your face (lose 2 ENDURANCE points), forcing you back towards the ravening black wolf.

If you wish to stand and fight the wolf, turn to **120**.

If you choose to run into the blazing inferno, turn to **204**.

156

Tavig has stopped screaming long before you force

the hand to give up its prize and withdraw, gashed and bleeding, into the gloom of the tunnel. Tavig's body lies motionless at your feet. You stoop to close his sightless eyes and lay his sword upon his blood-stained chest, as is the custom in the land of Slovia when a warrior falls in battle.

If you decide to leave the body and continue, turn to **323**.

If you wish to search the body before you go, turn to **227**.

157

Snatching the seed from your tunic pocket, you hurl it at the plinth as hard as possible. There is a loud crack as the shell shatters, and a splash of bright flame engulfs the plinth. Soon the hand catches fire; it wriggles and squirms as the flames feed on its loathsome flesh and is soon obscured by a pall of acrid black smoke.

If you wish to stand back and wait for the flames to die down, turn to **128**.

If you decide to pass around the fire and enter the passage beyond, turn to **284**.

158

Gasping for air, you claw your way to the surface and swim for the rocky shore. Heaving yourself from the cold water, you crouch down, breathless and exhausted, beside a line of huge boulders, half-buried in the coal-black sand, and take stock of your belongings. You have lost two Items from your Backpack and all the food has been ruined by the tainted water (erase all Meals and two Backpack Items of your choice from your *Action Chart*).

No sooner have you managed to control your breathing than you hear the sound of scraping, as if some heavy weight were being dragged across the rocks to your left. A verticle crack appears in the surface of the nearest boulder and a sickly yellow light washes over you. It is not a boulder – you are staring at a huge eye.

If you wish to draw your weapon and attack the eye, turn to **265**.

If you wish to leap to your feet and escape towards the sheer rock base of Kazan-Oud, turn to **41**.

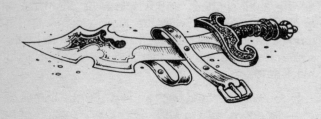

159

You walk upon the glittering marble flagstone of Zahda's throne-hall, your footsteps echoing among the circular tiers as you approach the central pit. The chamber is deserted and only the flickering flames that curl around the pinnacle of black iron shed any light upon the vastness.

'You dare to challenge the power of Zahda?' booms a voice in the darkness above, a voice made thunderous in the cavernous expanse of the throne-hall. A blinding white light holds you in its beam, blazing down from the throne with unnatural intensity. 'You dare to pit yourself against the Lord of Kazan-Oud?'

Desperately you try to escape from the beam but you cannot move. Your muscles are numb and nerveless, paralysed by Zahda's beam.

'I know your purpose – your identity was revealed to me in the maze. You are the Kai Lord – the one they call Lone Wolf.' The voice is now filled with anger and indignation. 'You have come here to steal that which belongs to me. For such a crime there can be only one penalty – death!'

A pulse of raw energy hurtles down from the throne, speeding towards you like a burning sun. It consumes you in a searing ball of flame, destroying you completely and forever.

Your life and your quest end here.

160

As the last enemy falls dead at your feet, a section of the wall slides back to reveal an ugly, bearded dwarf, wearing a grimy black velvet jerkin. His pig-like eyes twinkle malevolently as he raises a hollow brass tube and points it at your face.

'Sweet dreams,' he chortles, and a blast of icy-cold vapour shoots from the tip, catching you squarely in the face. You reel back, coughing and choking, as the bitter vapour fills your lungs. By the time your realize that you have inhaled a powerful sleep gas, you are already succumbing to its irresistible power.

Turn to **165**.

161

As the few remaining survivors whirl away into the darkness, you sheathe your weapon and kick aside the torn bodies of those who fell to your deadly blows. A stone room awaits you at the bottom of the stairs, featureless and bare except for a weapons' rack hanging on the wall in the far corner. It holds a Spear and a Broadsword, both in remarkably fine condition. The torchlit tunnels offer an exit from this chamber: one descends to the north, the other to the east.

If you wish to enter the north tunnel, turn to **187**.

If you wish to enter the east tunnel, turn to **101**.

If you have the Magnakai Discipline of Pathsman-ship, turn to **139**.

162

Your shot is fast and deadly accurate: the arrow pierces the warrior's armoured back just above the waist, pitching him forward on to his face. He writhes for a brief moment on the rubbish-strewn floor before surrendering to death.

Swiftly you race along the corridor, leaving the dead guard and the chamber far behind. You pass through an archway that opens out to a landing at the top of a spiral staircase and you descend the stairs. At the bottom of the stairs a tunnel leads off to the west and the east.

If you wish to go west, turn to **29**.

If you wish to go east, turn to **272**.

If you have the Magnakai Discipline of Pathsman-ship or Divination, turn to **171**.

163

You step through the green jadin arch and immediately a blistering wave of heat rises up through your body, burning you with agonizing pain. You have stepped into a portal of annihilation, and the last sound that you hear is the faint mocking laughter of Lord Zahda as he watches you walk to your doom from a platform high above the misty ceiling.

Your life and your quest end here.

164 – *Illustration IX (overleaf)*

You regain consciousness with a start, reaching instinctively for your weapon lest danger be waiting to greet you. A dull throbbing fills your head as you sit up to take stock of your surroundings.

You find yourself on top of a mound of rotting vegetation, stacked high in the corner of a shadowy chamber. A harsh reptilian odour fills your nostrils: the unmistakable smell of snakes. As your vision clears, you notice, amid the slime that covers the floor, what appear to be undigested human bones. A rib cage, two skulls and several vertebrae are illuminated by a shaft of light that descends from a grate in the ceiling. It flickers and, for a second, you catch a glimpse of a skull-like face through the iron bars. Fear wells up inside you as a chilling laugh pierces the silence. But it is not the sound of the cruel inhuman laughter that freezes your blood, it is the sight of the colossal, wedge-shaped head that is rearing up through the mound on which you sit; it is the head of a gigantic snake.

You leap to your feet and run to the far corner of the

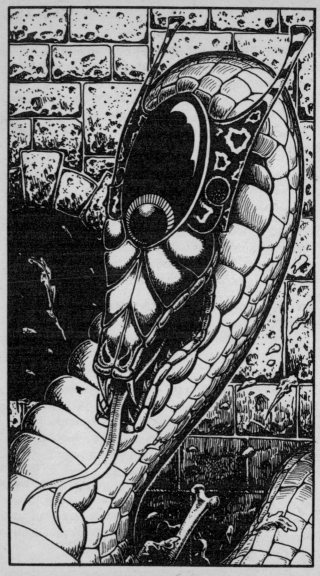

IX. The colossal, wedge-shaped head of a gigantic snake rears
up before you

chamber, your heart pounding loudly in your ears. The snake rises up almost to the ceiling, its forked tongue flickering angrily below a single yellow eye which is set deep in the centre of its green scaly head. Once more the chamber echoes to cruel laughter as the monster shakes off its rotting nest and slithers forward.

> If you have the Magnakai Discipline of Animal Control and have reached the Kai rank of Primate, turn to **137**.
> If you have a bow and wish to use it, turn to **7**.
> If you have neither a bow nor mastery of Animal Control, turn to **301**.

165 – *Illustration X (overleaf)*

You awake to such an astounding sight that you feel sure you must be dreaming. Before you lies a titanic, circular hall of glittering marble, rising tier on tier like a gigantic amphitheatre. A vast pit fills the centre, from which arises a pinnacle of black iron, which is licked by sheets of flame that roar up from the depths below. Scores of seated creatures crowd the tiers, every one of them staring at you, their eyes like pinpoints of fire gleaming coldly from the shadows of their hooded robes. You hear the rustle of their mocking laughter and your skin prickles with eerie premonition.

A great gong booms in the distance and a doleful chant arises from the crowded tiers. An urge to run from this evil place grips you like a fever but your wrists are manacled securely to a bronze ring fixed to the wall above your head.

'Let the trial commence!' commands a mighty voice, filling the hall with clamouring echoes. As one, the

X. Scores of seated creatures crowd the tiers, staring at you,
their eyes like pinpoints of fire

robed spectators rise from their seats as a shaft of light pours down upon the pinnacle, illuminating the outline of a man, white-haired and gaunt, seated on a massive throne of solid, gleaming gold. Suspended in the air above his head are two crystals: one as clear as a polished diamond; the other as black as the grave. A crackling arc of energy travels between the two and its flickering blue light sheds a ghostly shadow on the face of the seated lord.

'Intruder,' he says, his voice soft yet chilling, 'you have come to Kazan-Oud with murder in your heart. Have not the cowards of Elzian promised to reward you for my destruction?'

A drone of dissent surges from the crowded tiers, drowning any answer that you offer in your defence. The lord rises slowly from the throne and turns to his baying minions, his hands outstretched as if to receive the adulation. As their ghastly drone grows louder, your eye is drawn to the clear crystal that hovers above the throne. A golden light now glows at its core. In a flash of understanding you recognize the object of your quest: here is the Lorestone of Herdos.

'Your verdict, my children?' cries the wild-eyed man, his voice now harsh and angry.

'Guilty, Lord Zahda,' the crowd howls in reply.

'The sentence?' retorts their master.

'The maze!' they scream. 'The maze!'

If you possess the Sommerswerd, turn to **335**.
If you do not possess this Special Item, turn to **264**.

166

On your fifth step, the silence is broken by another crack. The invisible whip bites into the back of your legs, causing your knees to buckle, and you flinch with pain as you stagger forwards.

Pick a number from the *Random Number Table*. If you have the Magnakai Discipline of Huntmastery, add 2 to the number you have picked.

If your total is now *0–2*, turn to **275**.
If it is *3–7*, turn to **222**.
If it is *8* or more, turn to **311**.

167

You sense that a trap guards this portal; should you choose the wrong number, or numbers, before pulling the lever, the consequences could be fatal.

Turn to **329**.

168

The water is still pouring from the statue's face, although the pressure has dropped dramatically now that the chamber is nearly full. The entire face has crumbled away under the pressure of the water, leaving a hole the size of a dinner plate. Peering inside, you can see a large nozzle and a lever, both deep within the body, beyond arm's reach.

If you have a sword or a spear, turn to **32**.
If you do not have either of these weapons, turn to **263**.

169

The descending wall is gathering speed at a terrifying pace; there is now very little space left through which to escape.

Pick a number from the *Random Number Table*. If you have the Magnakai Discipline of Huntmastery, add 3 to the number you have picked.

If your total is now *0–4*, turn to **237**.
If it is 5 or more, turn to **326**.

170

Suddenly there is a flash of blinding light followed by a tremendous explosion. The creature is torn to pieces, consumed by a fireball of blistering yellow flame. The intense heat sears your face and hair (lose 4 ENDURANCE points) and hurls you backwards through the air. Shocked and stunned, you drag yourself into the fissure that is now illuminated by the remains of the monster that lie scattered and burning all around you.

Turn to **16**.

171

Your Kai mastery reveals that the wall at the bottom of the stairs conceals a secret door. One of the bricks is far smoother than the others and you sense that it activates the lock which keeps the door closed.

If you wish to press the brick, turn to **14**.
If you prefer to follow the tunnel to the west, turn to **29**.
If you prefer to take the tunnel to the east, turn to **272**.

172

You are washed out of the chamber and deposited on the floor of a corridor at the bottom of a steep ramp. Blinking the water from your eyes, you gaze with trepidation at your surroundings. The walls of the corridor, festooned with what appear to be gigantic cocoons, stretch into the distance as far as you can see. The oval door clicks shut and the click reverberates down the corridor, growing louder and louder. In the gloomy corridor ahead you see that something is moving.

A huge worm-like creature with great black eyes and horny mandibles is slithering towards you, a purple froth bubbling from its mouth as it fastens on your scent.

If you have the Magnakai Discipline of Invisibility, turn to **86**.

If you have the Magnakai Discipline of Animal Control and you have reached the Kai rank of Primate, turn to **130**.

If you have a Silver Whistle, turn to **347**.

If you have neither these skills nor the Special Item, turn to **233**.

173

The frenzied squeal of the rats fills your ears as you force your aching legs to propel you across the beach. Beyond an outcrop of pitted stone, a stream cascades down the sheer rock wall, cutting a deep gully across the beach as it flows into the lake. Spanning this gully is a natural bridge of stone. Its centre is very thin and narrow and, as you near the bridge, you fear it is too thin to support your weight.

If you wish to cross the narrow stone bridge, turn to **243**.

If you decide to try to swim across the gully, turn to **108**.

If you have the Magnakai Discipline of Divination, turn to **89**.

Blue fire leaps from Zahda's staff but you intercept and deflect it upon the blade of the sun-sword. The murderous bolt screams into the dark hall, destroying a whole tier of seats with a thunderous concussion.

'You will die . . . die . . . DIE!' shrieks Zahda like a man possessed. He whirls his staff twice about his head before lunging at your face with its clawed tip. Lord Zahda is immune to Mindblast and Psi-surge.

Lord Zahda (with power-staff):
COMBAT SKILL 33   ENDURANCE 45

If you win the combat, turn to **149**.

175

A pall of thick smoke spreads towards you from the body of the creature you have already killed, and your enemies use it to mask their advance. You steel yourself for a shot, but your aim is greatly hindered by the acrid fumes that are making your eyes stream and your throat tighten.

Pick a number from the *Random Number Table*. Unless you have the Magnakai Discipline of Weapon-mastery with bow, or the Magnakai Discipline of Nexus, deduct 3 from the number have picked.

If your total is now 5 or lower, turn to **19**.
If it is 6 or more, turn to **314**.

176

Slowly and carefully you advance, your eyes straining to see in the gloom. Ahead you notice that the tunnel takes a sharp left turn, but before you can reach the corner, you are frozen in your tracks by a blood-curdling howl that echoes from the vault behind. Spinning round, you stare aghast at the outline of a gigantic black wolf loping along the passage towards you. It moves at a terrifying pace, its evil eyes glowing scarlet and its great fanged jaws wide open in readiness to bite.

If you wish to stand and fight this ravening wolf, turn to **8**.
If you decide to turn the corner and run as fast as you can, turn to **140**.

177

The relief is instantaneous. Quickly you move from one stone to the next until you arrive at the shadowy opening in the wall. Echoing in the darkness, you hear the rustle and slither of unseen things. Suddenly something round and black breaks through the surface of the lake splitting the night with its hideous cry. It hovers for a few seconds above the water before hurtling towards you at an unnerving speed.

If you wish to take cover inside the fissure, turn to **16**.

If you wish to draw a weapon and prepare for combat, turn to **342**.

If you have a bow and wish to use it, turn to **225**.

178

Blindly, the young serpents writhe around your feet, their fanged jaws snapping wildly at your unarmoured legs. Combat is unavoidable and you must fight them as one enemy.

If you possess a Fireseed and wish to use it, turn to **191**.

Hactaraton Brood:
COMBAT SKILL 15   ENDURANCE 28

Unless you have the Magnakai Discipline of Curing, double all ENDURANCE point losses you sustain in the combat due to the venomous bite of these creatures.

If you win the combat, turn to **346**.

179

Your discipline blocks the psychic assault and eases the pain in your head, but the hand senses your resistance and tries a new form of attack. It curls its fingers, forming a grotesque fist, and pounds the plinth repeatedly with slow, heavy blows. Waves of psychic shock buffet your Psi-shield, forcing you to draw on all your strength just to keep the shield from collapsing.

> If you have the Magnakai Discipline of Psi-surge and have also reached the Kai rank of Primate, turn to **134**.

> If you do not have the power of Psi-surge, or if you have not yet reached the rank of Primate, turn to **297**.

180

Drawing on the power of your Kai skill, you take a deep breath and give voice to a single, unbroken tone. Sweat breaks out on your forehead as you raise the pitch of your voice steadily until it passes beyond the range of your own hearing. Suddenly, the bats shriek in unison. They twist and shudder, hurling themselves into the walls and ceiling as your cry paralyses their senses. As the few survivors whirl away into the darkness, you cease your call and hurry down the stairs. (If you used the Magnakai Discipline of Psi-surge, you need not deduct any ENDURANCE points from your current total.)

Turn to **236**.

181

The patrol comes to a halt less than ten feet from where you are hiding. The leader grunts an order and one of the black-clad armoured guards takes a flint from his pocket. He strikes it and sets light to a tar-coated torch fixed to the wall. The torch splutters into life and you are caught in the glare of its vivid yellow flame.

If you have a bow and wish to fire at the guards
before they react to your presence, turn to **206**.

If you wish to attack the guards with a hand
weapon, turn to **332**.

If you decide to run through the chamber and
attempt an escape into the opposite corridor,
turn to **69**.

182

You have no difficulty in looping your Rope around
the hilt of the sword and drawing it towards you. It is a
very plain, heavy-bladed weapon of poor quality and
unworthy of your scabbard, but in this strange and
hostile maze, this rough steel blade helps to restore
your hope of survival.

If you wish to leave the vault by the left tunnel, turn
to **298**.

If you prefer to take the right tunnel, turn to **322**.

183

No matter how hard you prod the slab it shows no
sign of movement, but your probing does uncover
something previously hidden beneath the dust. Carefully you scrape away the grime until the outline of a
coiled snake is revealed, etched deep into the dull
grey marble. Carved in the centre of its scaly coils is
the number **123**. Make a note of this number in the
margin of your *Action Chart* – it could be of use at a
later stage of your adventure.

If you wish to jump across the slab and press on
into the tunnel beyond, turn to **127**.

If you decide to enter the tunnel by walking across
the slab, turn to **277**.

184

Your lungs feel as if they are about to explode, but still the door will not open.

If you have a Vial of Blue Pills, turn to **230**.
If you wish to continue to try to open the door with your Magnakai discipline, turn to **313**.
If you wish to swim to the surface, turn to **153**.

185

A hollow sound, like the clatter of horses' hooves on cobblestones, arrests you in mid-step. Your basic Kai skills warn you that more of these evil creatures are running along the tunnel, heading in your direction. To proceed further would be suicidal. Over two hundred yards of narrow walkway separate you from the opposite tunnel, and as you turn and run you pray that you reach it before the Dhax appear. Pick a number from the *Random Number Table*.

If the number you have picked is *0–8*, turn to **241**.
If it is *9*, turn to **106**.

186

As you strike the killing blow, your enemy cries out in agony, materializing as he falls at your feet. At first glance, he appears to be human but as you search the body you discover otherwise. His eyes, now glazed and lifeless, are cat-like in structure; his fingers are short and tipped with claws; and his lower jaw protrudes several inches below his upper jaw. The skin is badly scarred but not by battle wounds; these are the scars of crude surgery.

There is no sign of the whip with which he attacked you, but you find a spear slung by a cord over his shoulder, and a Silver Whistle (mark this on your *Action Chart* as a Special Item) on a chain around his blood-spattered neck. Instinctively, you place the whistle to your lips and blow but there is no sound. Shaking your head, you turn to face the pit, and there before you, spanning the blackness, is a solid beam of blue metal.

If you wish to cross the beam, turn to **6**.

If you choose to retrace your steps along the corridor, turn to **64**.

187

The tunnel descends to a vast, cavernous hall. Spirals of yellow smoke rise up on either side of a narrow stone walkway that leads to its centre. There it meets another path running from east to west. Cautiously you advance along the walkway, your stomach unsettled by the stench of the sulphurous smoke and the sight of the dark, yawning void on either side.

At the junction, you hear the sound of running feet echoing from an archway to your right. The footfalls grow louder and, suddenly, a man in leather armour bursts out of the darkness, his studded boots striking sparks on the stone pathway as he skids to a halt. Sweat pours down his lean and leathery face, and his eyes flash with fear. He casts an anxious glance over his shoulder before unsheathing his sword and advancing towards you.

If you have a bow and wish to fire at the warrior, turn to **79**.

(continued over)

If you wish to draw your weapon and prepare to defend yourself, turn to **95**.

If you have the Magnakai Discipline of Divination, turn to **205**.

188

You dive through the gap, with barely an inch to spare, and the wall slams down behind you with a tremendous crunch. You lie flat on your back, your heart pounding fit to burst; your stomach churning at the thought of how near you came to death. Wearily, you get to your feet and press on along the tunnel, which is now noticeably cooler and clearer than before. You soon emerge into a hall that is filled with a strong, earthy smell. Two rows of great stone pillars support the roof and a huge granite sarcophagus stands in the centre of the floor. From the black entrance of a tunnel to your right, you hear the clanking of armour and the sound of approaching footsteps.

If you wish to hide behind one of the pillars, turn to **110**.

If you wish to leave the hall by a tunnel to your left, turn to **201**.

If you decide to lie in ambush for whoever or whatever it is that is approaching the hall, turn to **319**.

189

You duck and weave to present a difficult target to your enemy, but at such short range it is difficult for him to miss. The bolt hits you as you are diving forward, passing right through your skull and killing you instantly.

Your life and your quest end here.

190

The tentacle shudders as you direct the full power of your psychic discipline at the huge, wounded eye. Its grip weakens and you seize the chance to tear yourself free and scramble to your feet. The use of your Magnakai Discipline has cost you 2 ENDURANCE points, but it has saved you from a ghastly death. Make the necessary adjustments to your *Action Chart*.

Turn to **41**.

191

You grab the Fireseed from your pocket and hurl it to the ground. It explodes on impact with a blinding flash. Hissing and spitting, the serpent brood slither away into the shadows, eager to escape the stinging pain of the flames.

More noises echo from the chamber. This time it is the chinking of armour and weapons.

Turn to **346**.

192

You recognize the symptoms of takadea, or 'gaol-rot' as it is commonly called in your country. As you approach the trembling man, you reassure him that you mean him no harm, that you can help him if only he will trust you. Placing your hands over his eyes, you transfuse the healing power of your Magnakai skill into his sick body, concentrating your energy into reversing the terrible effects of the disease. When you remove your hands, his eyes are no longer opaque; they gleam with a cat-like intensity.

'I can see,' he says in astonishment, his voice cracked with emotion. 'How can I ever repay you for this miracle?' Before you can answer, the sound of running feet echoes along the corridor outside.

'Follow me,' he says, springing to his feet. 'If Zahda's guards find you in here they'll kill us both.'

Turn to **290**.

193

The staircase seems to continue forever, coiling its way upwards through the solid rock, but eventually you arrive at a landing from which a tunnel stretches into darkness. You are about to enter, when your basic Kai instincts alert you to a shallow step that crosses from one side of the tunnel to the other. A closer look reveals the step to be a perfect square of marble that covers the first ten feet of the tunnel floor.

If you wish to prod the marble slab with a weapon to test for a trap, turn to **183**.

If you wish to jump across the slab into the tunnel beyond, turn to **127**.

If you decide to enter the tunnel by walking across the slab, turn to **277**.

194

Wiping the gore from your face and hands, you fight back the nausea that rises in your throat when you think of how close you came to a grisly death in the jaws of the monster. The dim light grows suddenly brighter and, for a moment, you hear laughter, cold and distant, before the light dims once more to its usual murky glow and silence descends.

Turn to **322**.

195

Suddenly the corridor echoes to the clangour of an alarm bell. A solid sheet of iron crashes down from the ceiling to seal off the chamber behind you and, in the murky distance, you see a similar barrier descending in front of the wooden door by which you entered.

Turn to **37**.

196

The arrow whistles through the air towards the oncoming sphere. Impact looks imminent until the black ball suddenly changes course, darting aside at the last possible moment to avoid the missile. The arrow splashes harmlessly in the lake and you are forced to shoulder your bow and draw a hand weapon, as the menacing sphere resumes its attack.

> If you wish to stand and fight this object, turn to **342**.
>
> If you decide to evade its attack by moving deeper into the fissure, turn to **16**.

197

Using every scrap of cover to hide your passing, you move through the chamber like a phantom. As soon as you set foot into the corridor beyond, you are confronted by an armoured guard. He screams a cry that is muffled by the visor of his black helmet, and turns and runs towards a bell-rope that hangs from a hole in the ceiling.

> If you have a bow and wish to use it, turn to **266**.
>
> If you do not have a bow, or do not wish to use it, turn to **40**.

198 – *Illustration XI*

Suddenly you realize the horrific purpose of the hand. It is a predator, an evil sentient being that can only survive by consuming one form of nourishment – live human brain.

Diving and rolling, you avoid its initial attack, escaping with scratches to your scalp (lose 2 ENDURANCE points), but as it rises above you once more you cannot help but fear that your life is soon to end. This creature is immune to Mindblast, but *not* Psi-surge in combat.

Rahkos: COMBAT SKILL 18   ENDURANCE 30

If you win the combat, turn to **22**.

XI   The hand is a predator – it can only survive by consuming
live human brain

199

You recognize the dead man's hauberk as that of a Kakush mercenary: the ten-pointed star of Nikesa, the symbol of that country's capital city, adorns each of the rusty buckles that fasten his chain-mail armour. In a leather pouch hanging from his belt you discover 6 Gold Crowns, and inside the tattered remains of his Backpack, there is a Rope and a hooded Red Robe.

A close examination of the weapons shows them both to be quite useless: the bone-handled dagger crumbles to dust when you try to dislodge it from the corpse's skull, and the blade of the sword is dull and eaten by rust.

If you now wish to continue along the tunnel, turn to **318**.

If you decide to climb the stairs and investigate the open trap door, turn to **93**.

200

Chunks of stone and iron are blasted into the upper reaches of the throne-hall by the increasing power of the eruptions. Boulders, some the size of horses, seem to tumble in slow motion all around the beam as you are drawn irresistibly nearer to the roof. Suddenly the beam fades and you find yourself standing on a circular plinth in the centre of a ruined temple near to the gatehouse of the castle keep. The glare of daylight blinds you, but as you gradually become accustomed to it you cast your eyes over the shimmering waters of Lake Khor to the town of Herdos, perched on the horizon. The walls of the fortress are beginning to crack and slant. Buildings are crumbling and the ground is alive with constant vibration. You run through the ruined main gate as bolts of lightning are drawn from the sky by the dying power of Kazan-Oud.

At the top of a ruined staircase you stare down at the lake far below.

If you wish to descend the steps to the old jetty, turn to **122**.

If you choose to make your way to the beach, turn to **309**.

If you decide to dive from the cliff into the water far below, turn to **254**.

201

You make your way quickly along the tunnel until you reach a chamber illuminated by a shaft of shimmering red light that descends from a square hole in the ceiling. A pair of huge iron doors fills the opposite wall but in order to reach them you will have to pass through the eerie red light. Close to the archway by which you entered, another tunnel exits from the chamber, curving off towards the east.

If you wish to walk through the red light to examine the iron doors, turn to **269**.

If you wish to leave the chamber by the east tunnel, turn to **272**.

202

A howling blue fire leaps from Zahda's staff and instinctively you hurl yourself to the floor to evade its searing heat. The bolt screams past into the darkness of the hall, where it explodes in a splash of vivid sparks.

203

Zahda screams with anger and frustration and attempts to crush your head with one vicious blow, but you save yourself by rolling aside, and the staff cleaves open the black iron floor. A gout of flame rises from the split and blisters the mad lord's hand; he shrieks like a wounded crow and the staff drops from his fire-blackened fingers.

You see your chance to attack and lash out, but Zahda is quick to react. He leaps backwards, unsheathing a glowing dagger as he steadies himself on the brink of the abyss. Lord Zahda is immune to Mindblast but *not* Psi-surge.

Lord Zahda: COMBAT SKILL 25 ENDURANCE 45

If you win the combat, turn to **149**.

203 – *Illustration XII*

With your trembling hands clasped tightly around the slippery green rope, you fight to lock your feet together to prevent yourself from sliding into the heaving swell. The crack of splintering wood fills the night as the coracle shatters and sinks without trace. A sudden jolt runs the length of the rope and a snaky head rises from the black water. It dips and swerves upwards, opening its jaws, set with fangs like long yellow knives, and fixing you with its blind white eyes. You are clinging to the body of a deadly Lekhor that is poised to strike.

If you wish to release your grip of this deadly serpent and dive into the water, turn to **325**.

If you wish to draw a weapon and defend yourself against its venomous attack, turn to **76**.

XII.   You are clinging to the body of a deadly Lekhor that is
poised to strike

204

The temperature grows higher with every step you take but, as the first flame washes over your body, you feel no heat or pain at all. The gout of flame feels cool and refreshing, like a breeze on a hot summer's day. You quicken your step and soon emerge from the heatless flames into the empty passage beyond.

Turn to **240**.

205

You sense that the man is petrified with fear. An aura of evil grows stronger by the second, radiating from the darkened archway like a terrible black heat. The evil is so strong that it blocks your discipline and you cannot be sure if the warrior is a friend or a foe.

If you wish to draw a weapon and prepare to defend yourself, turn to **95**.

If you wish to avoid a confrontation by running into the archway opposite, turn to **47**.

If you have a bow and wish to fire at the warrior, turn to **79**.

206

You aim and fire a fraction of a second later, hitting the leader in the chest. He tumbles backwards, knocked off his feet by the force of your arrow. His followers growl their anger, unsheathing long knives and axes as they press forward to wreak their revenge.

Zahda Beastmen:
COMBAT SKILL 28   ENDURANCE 35

If you win the combat in three rounds or less, turn to **17**.

If combat lasts longer than three rounds, turn to **160**.

207

The key fits perfectly. You turn it and the door gives way instantly, forced wide open by the huge weight of water pressing upon it.

Turn to **172**.

208

The trunk tumbles into the gap, followed by a deluge of rock and rubble. As the dust clears, you find yourself still staring at the staircase above.

If you have a Rope, turn to **310**.
If you do not possess a Rope, turn to **211**.

209

Your killing blow makes the Oudagorg twist back on itself, its head disappearing into the misty ceiling. There is a deafening crack as blue lightning engulfs its neck, crackling snake-like around its horrible body and filling the corridor with the smell of burning meat. The creature thrashes wildly for several minutes, and when its gruesome dance finally ends you see that the canopy of mist is no longer there. In the darkness above you see a deserted walkway and a metal observation platform.

If you wish to climb on to the body of the dead Oudagorg and pull yourself on to the platform, turn to **294**.
If you wish to climb over the worm-like carcass and continue along the corridor, turn to **46**.

210

Once more you call on your Kai mastery to save you from reptilian threat, and once more it proves effective. The snakes turn away and slither to the safety of their nest, repelled by your presence as if the sight of you were as repulsive to them as the sight of them is to you.

Turn to **346**.

211

The only way you can cross the gap is by climbing the rock wall. However, the surface is virtually sheer, and any attempt to climb it without proper equipment would be perilous in the extreme.

If you wish to attempt such a climb, turn to **85**.
If you decide to descend the stairs and continue along the beach, turn to **348**.

212

As the Beastman crashes to the floor, two more come rushing in from the cell compound. They growl with anger at the sight of their dead comrade-in-arms, and launch themselves in a fearsome attack.

Beastman Gaoler No. 1:
COMBAT SKILL 17   ENDURANCE 23
Beastman Gaoler No. 2:
COMBAT SKILL 16   ENDURANCE 21

If you win the combat, turn to **80**.

213

There is a click and the panel slides open to reveal the small, dimly lit interior of the sarcophagus. A set of stairs descends to a strong wooden door that is reinforced with strips and studs of iron.

If you wish to enter the sarcophagus, turn to **37**.
If you decide not to enter, turn to **102**.

214

The iron door is several inches thick and will demand a tremendous effort to raise it high enough off the floor for you to escape underneath it.

To raise the door follow the normal combat rules as if you were unarmed (subtract 4 points from your COMBAT SKILL total). If you have the Magnakai Discipline of Nexus, you need not deduct any points from your COMBAT SKILL score. Any ENDURANCE points that you lose during this 'combat' represent the fatigue you suffer as you strain to lift the heavy door.

Tunnel Door:
COMBAT SKILL 19   ENDURANCE (Resistance) 50

You may cease 'combat' at any time and explore the tunnel instead; turn to **277**.

If you reduce the door's resistance (ENDURANCE) to 0, turn to **114**.

215

As you peer at the horrible hand, it suddenly leaps at your face. You scream with terror, instinctively lashing out to deflect its attack. You strike it hard and send it spinning towards the green pillars and the passage beyond. Just as it draws level with the pillars the hand explodes: it has spun straight into an invisible barrier of destructive energy that flows between the pillars.

As the hand disintegrates into thousands of tiny fragments you feel elated that, at last, victory is yours.

Turn to **334**.

216

To your relief you discover that the door is unlocked and unguarded. Beyond it, a torchlit corridor descends through a series of deserted chambers, each one defaced by years of neglect and decay. Rotting curtains and mouldering furniture are all that remain of a sumptuous abode, a luxurious underground retreat for the Lord of Kazan-Oud.

You are about to enter another of these chambers when the sound of muttering stops you dead in your tracks. Three spindly limbed creatures are seated at a table in the centre of the room. They chatter excitedly in a language that is alien to your ears, and point with slim, green fingers at a parchment spread out before them. They wear long, hooded robes of purple silk and appear to be unarmed.

If you have completed the Lore-circle of Solaris, turn to **244**.

If you wish to launch a surprise attack on these unsuspecting creatures, turn to **295**.

If you wish to try to sneak through the chamber and attempt to reach the opposite corridor unseen, turn to **343**.

217

The strength of your Kai mastery overcomes the pain that tears at your mind, and you swiftly regain full control of your body. Snatching up your weapon from the hot black sand, you lash out at the tendril, severing its tip. But instead of blood, or what would pass for blood in the body of this ghastly creature, a flame sparks into life like a spluttering fuse. The brain ceases to move, hovering motionless above the sand, as the spitting flame burns fiercely along its thin tube of sundered flesh.

Turn to **170**.

218

The first bubble bursts with a loud bang that causes the creature to howl with fear. You watch as the great black hound scrambles to a halt, its horrible face lined with fear. Whimpering pitifully it backs slowly up the corridor. At the corner it howls with frustration before slinking away out of sight.

Turn to **151**.

219

You lash out at the monster's eyelid and open a terrible wound. But before you can deal another blow, a bolt of red fire screams down from the grating, hits your shoulder, and paralyses your whole arm with a sickening pain. You reel back, your weapon clattering to the ground as your fingers are robbed of all feeling (lose 6 ENDURANCE points).

The snake writhes and twists in blind rage, its open jaws seeking you out to exact its revenge. It soon picks up your scent and attacks with frightening speed.

Giant Hactaraton:
COMBAT SKILL 20   ENDURANCE 45

220

Your weapon lies on the ground near your feet and you must deduct 4 points from your COMBAT SKILL total for the first two rounds of combat. If you are still alive at the beginning of the third round, you can retrieve your weapon. Unless you have the Magnakai Discipline of Curing, double all ENDURANCE points that you lose during the combat, due to the venomous bite of your enemy.

If you win the fight, turn to **21**.

220

Your companion rolls the body over and unsheathes a Short Sword and a Dagger from the belt. You may take the Axe that was used in combat and the Dagger, if you wish.

At the bottom of the stairs is a deserted hallway at the end of which are two great doors of gleaming bronze. Sumptuous tapestries and statuettes of gold line the walls on either side, and an ornate fountain of silvered marble fills the hall with a melodious bubbling sound.

You have covered less than twenty feet when an armoured guard steps into view from behind the fountain. He raises a crossbow and you shout a warning to your new-found partner – but you are too late. The bolt hisses through the air, hitting him with such force that he is knocked off his feet and sent crashing to the ground. The guard fumbles in a leather pouch for another quarrel with which to despatch you.

If you wish to aid your wounded companion, turn to **28**.

If you decide to attack the guard before he can reload his weapon, turn to **81**.

221 – *Illustration XIII (overleaf)*

A great toad-like face stares unblinkingly into your eyes as it emerges from the shadows to bask in the green light that illuminates the beach. Its body, pale and bloated like a huge, fat worm, slithers into view, and you shudder at the sight of the open sores that disfigure its skin.

A ghastly noise echoes from deep within its open mouth as it rears up to attack you with a razor-sharp tongue. Due to the surprise of its attack, you cannot make use of a bow.

Zagothal: COMBAT SKILL 29   ENDURANCE 28

If you wish, you may evade after two rounds of combat; turn to **229**.

If you have the Magnakai Discipline of Invisibility, you may evade combat at any time without losing ENDURANCE points; turn to **70**.

If you win the combat, turn to **271**.

222

You slip and fall but miraculously you manage to hang on to the invisible beam. Your legs are stinging (lose 2 ENDURANCE points) but you ignore the pain, concentrating all your effort on swinging them back on to the beam. Just as you succeed, the crack of the whip resounds once more and burns its mark across your back (lose another ENDURANCE point).

When the whip cracks a third time it cuts only air, for you have crawled out of range of its cruel bite.

Turn to **6**.

XIII.   A great toad-like face stares unblinkingly into your eyes

223

A searing current of pain runs the length of your arm and explodes in your head. Lights flash before your eyes and you collapse into unconsciousness.

Turn to **164**.

224

As your hand closes around the hilt of the sword, somewhere in the mist above your head the voice of the skull speaks a chilling rhyme:

> 'Hand to take;
> Spell to break;
> Stir a terror
> In your wake.'

If you still wish to pick up the sword, turn to **96**.

If you decide not to take the sword and wish to leave the vault by the left tunnel, turn to **298**.

If you prefer to leave by the right tunnel, turn to **322**.

225

Only the faint green light of the power-shield illuminates your moving target. You notch an arrow and take careful aim as it speeds up the beach, weaving in and out of the boulders that litter its path.

Pick a number from the *Random Number Table*. If you have the Magnakai Discipline of Weaponskill with bow, add 3 to the number you have picked.

If your total is now 0–6, turn to **196**.

If it is 7 or more, turn to **112**.

226

Without any warning, the hand springs to life. It stands upright on its fingers, the first two drawn back so that it resembles a monstrous spider preparing to attack. You step back aghast as it scurries around in a circle on the granite plinth.

If you wish to attack the hand, turn to **116**.

If you have a Fireseed and wish to throw it at the plinth, turn to **157**.

If you wish to skirt around the plinth and enter the passage beyond, turn to **302**.

227

His pack and the pockets of his leather armour contain the following items:

> Enough dried meat for 1 Meal
> Rope
> Blanket
> Dagger
> Vial of Blue Pills
> Bottle of Water
> Power-key

All the Items, with the exception of the Power-key, which is a Special Item, are Backpack Items. If you wish to take any of them, remember to adjust your *Action Chart* accordingly.

If you have the Magnakai Discipline of Curing, you can identify the nature of the Blue Pills by turning to **43**.

To leave the body and continue, turn to **323**.

228

The stone blocks crumble on the third blow and you waste no time climbing through the hole and into the rough-hewn tunnel beyond. The canopy of mist no longer obscures the ceiling and the tunnel is dark and damp; you feel sure that you have escaped from the maze.

The tunnel twists and turns like a gigantic snake until you arrive at a wall made up of planks of wood. The timber is rotten and you have no difficulty gaining access to the vaulted corridor beyond. The tunnel on this side of the wooden wall is far cleaner and drier, and you walk easily along it until you come to a junction: a passage crosses from left to right.

If you wish to take the passage to your left, turn to **20**.

If you wish to take the passage to your right, turn to **92**.

If you have the Magnakai Discipline of Paths-manship, turn to **330**.

229

Your heart pounding, you run as fast as you can towards the shelter of the rocky base of Kazan-Oud. Panting for breath, you reach the glistening black stone wall, where you discover a ragged fissure that splits its sheer surface. You are about to step in, when the rustle and slither of unseen things, echoing from the inky darkness makes you hesitate.

If you wish to enter the fissure, turn to **16**.

If you wish to press on along the beach, turn to **173**.

230

As soon as you swallow the pills, you feel your body relax and your lungs cease to ache. Oxygen is being drawn from the water around you, absorbed by your body through the pores of your skin.

Freed from the immediate threat of drowning, you apply yourself to finding a way out of this watery tomb.

> If you wish to try to open the locked door, turn to **66**.
>
> If you wish to examine the statue, turn to **168**.

231

There is a soft click and the panel slides open to reveal a set of steps leading down to a wooden door, its timber reinforced with bands of iron.

> If you wish to enter the sarcophagus, turn to **37**.
>
> If you decide against entering, turn to **102**.

232

Your arrow pierces the leading creature's arm. It staggers and howls abysmally as a thick, green fluid oozes from the wound. To your surprise and disgust, the others leap upon their injured companion, biting and clawing at the wound with their teeth and talons. The limb is swiftly torn from the body and consumed.

> If you wish to draw another arrow and fire again, turn to **152**.
>
> If you decide to shoulder your bow and evade these ghoulish creatures by escaping into the archway opposite, turn to **241**.

233

Relentlessly the worm moves forward, forcing you back up the ramp towards the oval door. But there is no escape this way – you have no choice but to fight the repulsive crature. The monster is especially susceptible to psychic attack. If you choose to use Mindblast or Psi-surge during combat, double all ENDURANCE point losses sustained by the enemy.

If you win the combat, turn to **209**.

234

You recognize the tangle of greyish-green weed half-submerged in the waters around your sinking boat. It is Black Lakeweed, a carnivorous plant commonly found in the swamps and freshwater lakes of central Magnamund. Forewarned by your Kai mastery, you dive into the lake and swim submerged until you are clear of the deadly plants.

Turn to **158**.

235

The hand is fast but you are faster. Diving and rolling, you avoid its initial attack and crouch ready to receive its next attempt. It rises once more and, as you stare at its ghastly form, you suddenly realize its horrific purpose. It is a predator, an evil, sentient being that can only survive by consuming an exclusive form of nourishment – live human brain. You fight back your rising fear as it speeds towards you. This creature is immune to Mindblast (but not Psi-surge) in combat.

Rahkos: COMBAT SKILL 18   ENDURANCE 30

If you win the combat, turn to **22**.

236

A stone room awaits you at the bottom of the stairs, featureless and bare except for a weapons rack hanging on the wall in the far corner. It holds a spear and a broadsword, both in remarkably fine condition. Two torchlit tunnels offer exits from the chamber; one descends to the north, the other to the east.

If you wish to enter the north tunnel, turn to **187**.
If you wish to enter the east tunnel, turn to **101**.
If you have the Magnakai Discipline of Pathsmanship, turn to **139**.

237

You dive and roll, but your Backpack hits the falling wall and jams. In the next instant you are crushed by twenty tons of solid stone.

Your life and your mission have come to a tragic end here.

238

Rolling the body over with the toe of your boot, you quickly check for useful Items and discover the following:

> AXE
> SHORT SWORD
> DAGGER
> 2 GOLD CROWNS

Remember to mark any Items you wish to keep on your *Action Chart* before making your escape down the stairs.

Turn to **55**.

239

The sharp crack of splintering wood fills your ears as
you are thrown bodily through the air. The stinking
cobblestones of the jetty greet your return to earth
and, instinctively, you roll on landing to lessen the
shock of impact. You are winded but otherwise
unharmed. Staggering to your feet, you see two
rough-hewn staircases at the far end of the jetty: one
ascends to a cave-like entrance in the sheer rock wall;
the other leads down to a tiny beach covered with
boulders and black sand.

If you wish to climb the staircase to the entrance
above, turn to **82**.
If you wish to descend to the beach below, turn to
30.
If you have the Magnakai Discipline of Pathsmanship, turn to **251**.

240

You cover fifty yards before the passage opens into a
large, circular chamber. There, on a plinth in the
centre of the floor, rests a severed human hand. The
skin is mottled and swollen, the fingers black and

decayed. Beyond the plinth, the passage continues straight ahead, flanked by two pillars of speckled green stone.

If you wish to examine the severed hand, turn to **226**.

If you wish to skirt around the plinth and enter the passage beyond, turn to **302**.

241

A bolt of red fire whistles past your head and explodes just above the archway. Fragments of rock graze your scalp and you are momentarily blinded as you run through the debris. As you raise your arm to wipe your face on your sleeve, another bolt catches you squarely in the back and pitches you flat on your stomach.

Pick a number from the *Random Number Table*. If you have the Magnakai Discipline of Curing, deduct 1 from this number. The resulting figure represents the number of ENDURANCE points you have lost due to the attack.

Fighting back the pain, you clamber to your feet and stagger into the dust-choked tunnel.

Turn to **277**.

242

You peer into the keyhole but cannot see beyond the plate that hides the mechanism. The water reaches your chin, submerging the lock completely, and you are forced to tilt back your head in order to breathe.

If you have the Magnakai Discipline of Nexus, turn to **327**.

If you do not have this skill, turn to **153**.

243

As you reach the centre of the bridge, the leading rats are flowing up the slope of the arch. You turn and confront them, drawing a weapon in preparation for a fight to the death, if necessary. As they swarm nearer, you lash out, cleaving them from the narrow apex to fall, splashing, into the torrent of water below.

With your third blow, a shudder runs through the stone, causing you to stagger and fall. You land on the opposite bank, winded but otherwise unharmed. A loud crack fills the night and the whole centre section of the bridge collapses into the gully with a tremendous splash. Safe now from the ravenous rats, you can afford to continue along the beach at a less punishing pace.

Turn to **23**.

244

Your mastery of this Lore-circle enables you to understand the creatures' strange language, and from the shadows of the entrance you listen intently to their conversation.

'Repairs in the central shaft are nearly finished. In three suns' time we will be able to continue,' comments a reedy voice.

'We cannot wait that long,' interrupts another, its voice deeper and angrier in tone. 'Lord Zahda ordered the tunnelling to begin again without delay. We must obey his command.'

'But the risks are too great,' retorts the first voice. 'We

lost a hundred slaves in the flood—next time we may lose more than just slaves.'

A noise in the corridor alerts you to approaching danger: a patrol of armoured guards is heading in your direction.

> If you wish to try to sneak through the chamber and attempt to reach the opposite corridor unseen, turn to **343**.
>
> If you wish to hide in the shadows of the doorway, turn to **181**.

245

The hound bounds forward and leaps at your chest, slamming you to the ground with its monstrous weight. Its fangs flash before your eyes and a burning saliva stings your face. With all the strength you can muster you fight desperately for survival.

The creature is immune to Mindblast (but not Psi-surge).

Hound of Death:

COMBAT SKILL 22   ENDURANCE 40

If you win the combat, turn to **259**.

246

Your command works: the pain quickly subsides. However, the creature's rubbery tendril is still drawing closer to your vulnerable throat. Snatching up your weapon from the hot, black sand, you lash out and sever the tip, but instead of blood, or what would pass for blood in the body of this ghastly creature, a flame sparks into life like a spluttering fuse. The brain ceases to move, hovering motionless above the sand, as the spitting flame burns fiercely along the thin tube of flesh.

Turn to **170**.

247

'You need not fear me,' you say, trying to calm the frightened man. 'I will not harm you.'

The sound of your voice stops him shaking. He turns his scarred face towards you and asks, 'Have the Elder Magi sent you here?'

If you wish to answer the man, turn to **340**.

If you wish to leave the cell without answering his question, turn to **142**.

248

Before your last defeated enemy hits the ground, you are sprinting along the corridor, anxious to leave the chamber and the dying guards far behind. You pass through an archway that leads on to an open landing at the top of a spiral staircase, and hurry down. At the bottom, a tunnel leads off to the west and the east.

If you wish to go west, turn to **29**.

If you wish to go east, turn to **272**.

If you have the Magnakai Discipline of Paths-manship or Divination, turn to **171**.

249 – *Illustration XIV (overleaf)*

Snickering with evil delight, the creatures stalk closer and closer. Talons spring from the fingers of their leathery, webbed hands and their eyes blaze with wild red fire as they prepare to pounce.

Dhax: COMBAT SKILL 27   ENDURANCE 35

(continued over)

XIV. Snickering with evil delight, the Dhax stalk closer and closer

You may evade after three rounds of combat by
running into the archway opposite; turn to **241**.
If you win the combat, turn to **141**.

250

You close your hand around the Lorestone of
Herdos and your senses reel as a wave of energy
washes over your body (restore your current
ENDURANCE points score to its original total). Your
senses tingle and a new-found strength wipes away
the fatigue of your terrible ordeal, enabling you to
assess the situation anew. A vibration runs through
the iron floor, a forewarning of the eruptions that will
tear Kazan-Oud to pieces. Swiftly you descend the
spiral stairs and sprint along the tube, oblivious of the
heat and noise that buffet you mercilessly as you run
towards the distant hall. There, you find everything in
chaos: Zahda's minions, his guards and his slaves run
in blind confusion as they try to escape from the
impending doom.

If you wish to fight your way up the stairs to the
prison cell complex level, and try to escape from
there, turn to **300**.

If you choose to ignore the stairs and follow the
corridor on this level, turn to **315**.

If you have the Magnakai Discipline of Paths-
manship or Divination, turn to **338**.

251

You can see the faint outline of stepping stones,
stretching across the beach to a narrow crack in the
rock wall. You sense that there is an entrance there.

If you wish to descend to the beach and investigate
further, turn to **303**.

(continued over)

If you decide to climb the staircase to the entrance above, turn to **82**.

252

It takes several minutes of continuous probing and twisting with the tip of your sword to persuade the plate to slide across, but still the door does not open. The effect of the pills is beginning to wear off now and the pain is slowly returning to your chest.

If you wish to continue to probe the lock with your sword, turn to **4**.

If you choose to abandon the door, only the statue offers any hope of escaping from this chamber; turn to **168**.

253

Swiftly you take aim and fire, but the creature escapes with just a graze across its dog-like forehead. Screaming with fury, it hurtles along the walkway and throws itself, clawing and snapping, at your face. You drop your bow and unsheathe a weapon just in time to receive its attack.

Dhax: COMBAT SKILL 20   ENDURANCE 26

You may evade combat at any time by running into the archway opposite; turn to **277**.

If you win the combat, turn to **141**.

254

You dive straight and true, avoiding the bodies that float on the surface, and enter the water at a perfect angle. Unfortunately, the water is scalding hot – fissures of molten lava have erupted through the brittle crust of the shallows. You scream all the way to the surface, but the shock paralyses your limbs and you sink like a stone shortly afterwards.

Tragically, your life and your mission end here.

255

A number of trees were unearthed by the falling tower, and one of them lies balanced precariously over the edge of the rock wall above. You focus your Kai mastery on this trunk and, after great mental exertion, you cause it to topple over the edge. As it crashes down the stairs, you fight to steer it end over end so that it comes to rest across the gap. But it gathers speed too quickly and is soon falling out of control.

Pick a number from the *Random Number Table*. If your current ENDURANCE points total is 20 or more, add 2 to the number you have picked.

If your total is now *0–2*, turn to **154**.
If it is *5–8*, turn to **208**.
If it is *9* or more, turn to **52**.

256

A dark corridor greets you beyond the door. You enter and feel your way along the wall, guided only by a tiny light in the distance. The sudden screech of metal sends a chill down your spine and, to your horror, you see a wall of black iron falling in front of the door.

Turn to **37**.

257

Another crack cuts the air, and you flinch as the invisible whip draws a crimson line across your thigh (lose 2 ENDURANCE points). You strain your Kai senses trying to discover the location of your enemy, but the magic that shields him is very strong.

Unless you have the Magnakai Discipline of Huntmastery, reduce your COMBAT SKILL by 2 points for the duration of the fight. If you possess a Blanket or a Red Robe, you may wrap it around your arm as extra protection from the blows of your enemy (it will increase your COMBAT SKILL by 1 point).

Invisible Whipmaster:
COMBAT SKILL 24   ENDURANCE 26

You may evade combat after three rounds by running back along the passage; turn to **64**.

If you win the fight, turn to **186**.

258

The faint green glow of the power-shield is the only source of light in the cave. Cautiously you advance but you are soon swallowed up by the darkness and progress becomes painfully slow.

If you have a Kalte Firesphere, a Lantern, or a Torch and Tinderbox, turn to **186**.

If you do not have any of these Items, and wish to continue ahead in total darkness, turn to **277**.

If you prefer to abandon the cave and return to the beach below, turn to **30**.

259

Wiping the dead wolf's blood from your eyes, you turn to face the floating bubbles that cluster in the corridor beyond.

If you wish to push your way past them, turn to **107**.

If you wish to cut a path through them with your
   sword, turn to **151**.
If you decide to retrace your steps to the vault and
   take the other tunnel, turn to **322**.

260

The tunnel reeks with the rancid odour of decay and,
to your dismay, you discover that it is no more than a
shallow cave – a shelter for a clutch of gigantic eggs,
each one as large as a barrel of ale. They rest upon a
bed of packs and torn clothing, belonging to previous
adventurers who fell foul of the giant snake.

If you wish to examine these Items more closely,
   turn to **148**.
If you wish to search for a way to escape from the
   tunnel, turn to **346**.

261

Both the skull and the echo of its voice gradually
disappear, to be replaced by the sound of heavy
footsteps approaching from the passage behind. The
gloomy corridor looks deserted but the footsteps are
growing louder and louder.

If you have a Flask of Wine or a Bottle of Water,
   turn to **18**.
If you have neither of these Items, turn to **304**.

262

The door is locked but the mechanism is so rusted
that it crumbles under the slightest pressure. Inside is
a squalid little room filled with barrels, crates and
dusty bottles of wine, all sour. On a damp wooden
bench lies a Short Sword, and beside it a plain circular

Shield (if you wish to take either of these Items, remember to mark them on your *Action Chart*; the Shield is a Special Item which adds 2 points to your COMBAT SKILL when used in combat).

If you wish to search the room further, turn to **73**.

If you decide to leave the room and explore the stairs, turn to **11**.

263

As your brain is starved of oxygen your vision grows dimmer, and you feel light-headed. Gradually the pain that burns in your chest fades away as unconsciousness smothers your senses. You sink slowly to the floor, weighed down by the water that now fills your lungs.

Your life and your quest end here.

264

The crowd howls its approval as a rickety, hunchbacked creature, swathed in a hooded robe, approaches the platform on which you stand manacled to the wall. Deftly he strips you of all your weapons and passes them to an ugly-faced dwarf, hovering close by his side.

'Take him to the maze,' commands the white-haired lord. His cruel, mocking laughter echoes in your ears as you are dragged from the hall in chains.

Erase all weapons and weapon-like Special Items from your *Action Chart* and make a note of them on a separate piece of paper in case you should rediscover them at a later stage of your adventure.

Now turn to **286**.

265 – *Illustration XV (overleaf)*

You plunge your weapon into the monstrous eye and gouts of a luminous jelly-like substance pour from the wound. A ghastly inhuman scream of pain rises from the ground beneath your feet. Jets of hissing steam erupt through the sand and a stinging cloud of grit assails your eyes.

You reel backwards, shielding your face from the blast, but an unexpected blow to your legs sends you sprawling to the ground (lose 2 ENDURANCE points). Before you can rise, a warty, green tentacle coils around your waist and pulls you slowly towards the mutilated eye.

If you have the Magnakai Discipline of Psi-surge, and wish to use it, turn to **190**.

If you do not possess this skill, or do not wish to use it, turn to **121**.

266

To prevent the guard from reaching the bell-rope you are forced to fire without taking careful aim.

Pick a number from the *Random Number Table*. If you have the Magnakai Discipline of Weaponmastery with bow, add 3 to the number you have picked.

If your total is now 6 or lower, turn to **75**.
If it is 7 or higher, turn to **162**.

267

You search the gleaming throne and the dais of black iron rock upon which it rests, and discover a pentacle carved deep into the gold. As you trace its design with your finger, a sound grows above the din of destruc-

XV.   You plunge your weapon into the monstrous eye and gouts of a luminous jelly-like substance pour from the wound

tion – a sound like the tinkling of a thousand tiny bells. In the blackness above the throne, a speckled glow appears. Slowly it descends towards you until a large section of the dais is engulfed by a column of shimmering blue light.

You reach up and a wave of energy surges through your body as you close your hand around the Lorestone of Herdos (restore your ENDURANCE points score to its original total). Your senses tingle and a new-found strength wipes away the fatigue of your terrible ordeal, enabling you to assess the situation anew.

The column of light is a magical transporter, a beam in which gravity has been reduced almost to zero. By entering it you will be drawn towards the surface level of Kazan-Oud.

Without hesitation you pocket the Lorestone and step into the magical beam.

Turn to **200**.

268

Simultaneously, you jump across the slab, rolling over as you hit the solid floor beyond. The creatures laugh horribly. They raise their sinewy arms and spread their webbed fingers, shooting forth their talons like curved assassins' knives. They lurch forward to attack, blinded by bloodlust to the danger that lies beneath their cloven hooves.

In an instant their laughter turns to lamentation as the slab drops away and they disappear, screaming as they plummet, into a deep, dark abyss.

Turn to **12**.

269

As the red light washes over you a tingling sensation passes through your body, leaving your muscles stiff and painful. Your limbs feel abnormally heavy and soon you have great difficulty putting one foot in front of the other. Suddenly the ground shakes and a large slab of stone rises from the floor to seal off the exit; a loud hissing fills your ears.

A strangely bitter smell assails your nostrils. By the time you realize that the air is being flooded with a powerful sleep gas, pumped from vents hidden in the ceiling, you are already succumbing to its irresistible power.

Turn to **165**.

270

A noise, like the sound of a thousand screeching cats, issues from the statue and water pours from its eyes and mouth. The stream quickly becomes a raging torrent and threatens to flood the chamber. You turn and run towards the passage, but, to your dismay, you find the passage is now sealed by a wall of solid stone.

With the water level at your waist, you wade across to the oval-shaped door and feverishly examine the lock.

If you have a Skeleton Key, turn to **207**.
If you do not have this Special Item, turn to **242**.

271

The hideous creature lets out a deafening cry as you strike your final blow. It crashes to the ground, displacing a ton of sand as its massive bulk settles on the beach. Attached to a heavy black chain around its loathsome midriff is a Gold Key. If you wish to take this Key, mark it on your *Action Chart* as a Special Item, which you keep in your pocket.

Your victory raises your spirits, but they soon sink again when you hear the unmistakable sound of rats – the chase has resumed.

Turn to **173**.

272

You follow the tunnel for nearly an hour before arriving at a torchlit hall, whose walls are hung with beautiful tapestries, undamaged by the damp that pervades the upper levels of the grim fortress. It looks as if the hall is a dead end and you are about to turn back when you notice a small door tucked away in one corner of the opulent chamber.

If you wish to open the door, turn to **256**.
If you prefer to take a closer look at the tapestries, turn to **305**.

273

A flood of armoured guards pours down the stairs, followed by a pair of hideous black-skinned, dog-faced creatures that wield long, glowing maces. You brace yourself for their assault, but they advance no closer. Instead the creatures make dreadful snickering sounds and raise their maces, tapping the ends together before simultaneously pointing them at you.

Suddenly you are torn with an agonizing pain, as your chest explodes in a gout of red flame. You topple backwards, your body almost rent in two by the bolt of destructive energy.

You have fallen victim to deadly Dhax power-staves and your life and your quest end here.

274

At first glance, the door looks completely smooth: no locks, bars, rivets or hinges mar its polished surface. However, a closer examination reveals a tiny keyhole set near to the floor.

If you have a Gold Key, turn to **333**.
If you do not possess this Special Item, turn to **54**.

275

You tumble into the pit and are swallowed up by total darkness. You fall at a terrifying speed for what seems an eternity and, after several minutes, you lapse into unconsciousness. It is a blessing, for you are spared the agonizing pain of being burnt alive when your body hits a lava pool ten thousand feet below.

Your life and your quest end here.

276

Silently you aim and fire. The arrow sinks feather-deep into the skull of the creature seated to your left. The others shriek with horror and surprise and leap from their seats, scrambling to take cover behind the table. Suddenly the clang of a bell fills the room, and the sound of running footsteps echoes along the corridor. Four warriors burst into the chamber, their weapons drawn, their bodies encased in shiny black armour. They take one look at the dead creature and hurl themselves at you in a frenzied attack.

If you wish to fire your bow again, turn to **50**.
If you decide to shoulder your bow and draw a hand weapon, turn to **316**.

277

You have taken only a few steps when you hear a faint whispering sound. You watch, horrified, as the hard stone floor beneath your feet disappears into a yawning black hole. Helpless, you tumble into the void, knocking yourself unconscious on a jagged outcrop of rock as you plummet into unknown depths.

Turn to **164**.

278

The creature launches itself at the cocoons, shearing them from the wall with its razor-sharp mandibles. The air is filled with fibrous shards and dust, and you no longer have a hiding place. You have no choice but to retreat along the corridor.

Turn to **233**.

279

In response to your psychic power, the sword rises from the block and glides towards your open hand. It is a plain, heavy-bladed weapon of poor quality and unworthy of your scabbard, but in this strange and hostile maze, this rough steel blade helps to restore your hopes of survival.

If you wish to leave the vault by the left tunnel, turn to **298**.

If you wish to leave by the right tunnel, turn to **322**.

280 – *Illustration XVI*

Tavig is barely visible inside the massive fist that is retreating down the tunnel. His screams, and the low rumbling growl of the monster that holds him, echo in your ears as you unsheathe your weapon and give chase. You must strike on the move if you are to break the monster's grip and save Tavig from a ghastly death.

Giant Fist: COMBAT SKILL 10   ENDURANCE 42

If you reduce the enemy's ENDURANCE score to zero in three combat rounds or less, turn to **291**.

If combat lasts four rounds or more, turn to **156**.

281

Pressing yourself flat against the tunnel wall, you draw on your skill to mask the warmth of your body. Nausea rises in your throat as the loathsome snakes slither across your feet and coil around your legs, but to them you are of no more interest than the cold and clammy stones that cover the tunnel floor. The snakes move on, leaving you shaken but unharmed.

Turn to **346**.

XVI.   Tavig is barely visible inside the massive fist that is
retreating down the tunnel

282

You hear footsteps on the stairs – more of the enemy are approaching. If they, too, are armed with cross-bows, your chances of survival will be very slim indeed. Before you stand two great bronze doors, flanked on either side by tapestries and gold statuettes.

If you wish to open the doors and enter, turn to **159**.

If you wish to examine the tapestries, turn to **74**.

If you decide to stand and fight the approaching enemy, turn to **173**.

283

The vast swarm reels back to feast upon the mutilated remains of their kin that lie piled in heaps all around you. Your arms, legs and hands are bleeding from several small nips and gashes, where one or more of the rats broke through your formidable defence to bury their chisel-like teeth into your skin. Your victory has bought you time to think, but it will be only a matter of seconds before the rats launch another attack.

If you wish to climb over the reef of jagged rocks to your left, turn to **336**.

If you decide to drag your coracle back into the water and escape from the bay, turn to **117**.

284

Covering your nose with your Kai cloak, you edge your way around the smoking flames and head towards the passage. As you step through the entrance, you walk straight into an invisible barrier, a field of destructive energy that flows between the two green pillars. With a thunderous concussion, you are repelled from the shield and sent tumbling back into the chamber (lose 8 ENDURANCE points; lose only 6 points if you have the Magnakai Discipline of Nexus).

If you are still alive, turn to **128**.

285

The bats are ravenously hungry and have been stirred to a frenzy by the unexpected smell of their favourite food – warm human blood. It is too late to avoid combat; you must fight for your life if you are not to become their feast.

Unless you have the Magnakai Discipline of Curing, you must double all ENDURANCE point losses you sustain during the fight, due to the bats' poisonous saliva.

Vampire Bats: COMBAT SKILL 19   ENDURANCE 32

If you win the combat, turn to **161**.

286

An escort of armoured guards forces you along a steel passageway lined by a crowd of jeering minions. They punch and spit as you pass between them, and their foul curses ring in your ears. The guards halt before a huge door of iron and unlock the manacles that encase your bruised and bloodied wrists. The points of their spears never wander far from your throat, discouraging any attempt at escape. The door rumbles open and a cheer goes up as you are pushed head first into a foul-smelling pit.

'Welcome to the maze,' sneers the chilling voice of Lord Zahda from somewhere high above your head. You struggle to your feet and peer up at a ceiling of swirling mist. A faint glow is gradually taking shape, condensing and forming into the likeness of a human skull. Baleful green eyes stare down at you from bony sockets, and a powdered wig, like that of a high court judge, sits squarely upon its fleshless head.

'You came here to kill but your plans have been foiled and now you must face the consequence,' echoes a voice in the skull. 'You have been sentenced to enter the Maze of Zahda. If you escape, your life may be spared; if you fail then you will surely die – a fitting end for one who came here in search of death.'

The skull retreats into the mist and a deathly silence fills the pit. A semi-circular shadow forms on the wall ahead; it grows larger and darker until it resembles the mouth of a cave or tunnel. Suddenly a gust of chill air whistles from out of this darkness and you realize that you are staring at the entrance to the maze.

'Enter!' orders the voice. 'Enter or die where you stand!' It is no idle threat. A crossbow bolt slams into the sand barely inches from your feet, and the click of a steel drawstring warns that another could follow if you disobey the command. Reluctantly, you step forward and enter the Maze of Zahda.

Turn to **111**.

287

Mustering all your reserves of strength, you spring along the passage, spurred on by the sound of gnashing fangs. There is a dead end ahead but a passage leads off to the right. You turn the corner as fast as you can, scraping the wall painfully with your shoulder as you fight to keep on your feet, but you are soon forced to a halt – the passage is blocked. Glinting in the dim light is a cluster of huge bubbles, floating languidly up and down between the misty ceiling and the polished floor. A slight breeze lifts them and they bounce towards you.

A snarl and the scraping of claws on stone tell you that the wolf is at the corner.

> If you wish to push through the bubbles and continue along the passage beyond, turn to **84**.
> If you wish to stand and fight the wolf, turn to **245**.
> If you decide to cut your way through the bubbles with your sword, turn to **218**.

288

Vivid green flashes of forked lightning and the rumble of distant thunder add menace to the towers and sheer stone walls of Kazan-Oud. Many of the roofs and turrets are in ruin; their twisted beams and floors lay open to the sky, giving the fortress a burnt-out and deserted appearance.

As you approach the tiny bay, which is tucked inside the shelter of a horseshoe reef of jagged black rocks, your eye is caught by the glow of tiny red lights, moving in the shadows at the base of the fortress wall. You notice a dry hollow among a group of rocks close to the shore that offers an ideal hiding place for your little boat. Silently, you disembark and drag the coracle up the beach towards the rocks. Seconds later you are halted dead in your tracks by the sound of muffled squealing. Sweat breaks out on your brow when a flash of lightning reveals scores of small red eyes close to the sand. A seething flood of rats, each as large as a puppy but gaunt and half-starved, is scurrying down the beach towards you like a torrent of black water.

With pounding heart, you search for some means of escape from this ravenous horde of squealing, snapping rodents.

> If you wish to climb over the rocks and escape across a deserted beach, turn to **336**.
> If you wish to drag your little boat back into the lake and paddle away from the bay, turn to **117**.
> If you prefer to stand and fight the onrushing flood of giant rats, turn to **45**.

Your light flares brightly in the moist gloom of the passage. A cavern lies immediately ahead, its high-arched roof a mass of dripping stalactites, hanging like thick spears of pearly white stone. Cautiously you step across the cavern floor, your skin prickling, as peculiar sounds emanate from the shadows.

You wind your way through a labyrinth of tunnels, slipping on moss-covered rocks, grazing your head on low ceilings and scrambling up and down steep ridges and rockfalls until you arrive at a smooth-walled chamber carved with precision from the hard black rock. A staircase ascends through an archway to your left, and directly ahead stands a massive stone door.

> If you wish to examine the stone door, turn to **274**.

If you wish to ascend the stairs, turn to **193**.

290

You follow him to the end of the cell block corridor, the angry shouts of Zahda's gaolers ringing in your ears. A staircase looms ahead, descending to a lower level, but it is guarded by a grim-faced Beastman, armed with an axe. Double all ENDURANCE points lost by your enemy during this combat for the Beastman is also being attacked by your new-found partner.

Beastman Gaoler:
COMBAT SKILL 17   COMBAT SKILL 22

If you win the combat, turn to **220**.

291

A terrible moan shakes the tunnel as your blows sever a finger from the monstrous hand. The others instantly spring open, dropping Tavig, bloodied and dishevelled, in a heap on the gore-stained floor. As the hand withdraws into the gloom, you kneel by Tavig's side and try to aid him as best you can. His injuries are severe; he is on the very brink of death.

If you have the Magnakai Discipline of Curing, turn to **133**.
If you do not possess this skill, turn to **125**.

292

The air becomes thinner, and slowly, painfully, you weaken and collapse. Consciousness soon fades and you are spared the agonies of death by suffocation.

Your life and your quest end here.

293 — *Illustration XVII*

Stealthily, you cross the cracked, flagstoned floor of the Great Hall, your muscles and nerves tensed for sounds of danger. The constant sound of dripping water and the howl of the storm adds to the utter desolation of the chamber. A thorny jungle of briars climbs the walls with greedy claws, coiling around the rotten frames of paintings and weaving through damp and mouldering tapestries.

Suspended above the fireplace is a great Anarian broadsword, its pitted steel blade pointing to one side. Your eyes travel along the blade to the shadows of the fireplace and you notice something lying in the grate. Moving nearer, you see that it is the body of a dead man. Behind it is a panel, wedged open by the corpse, and, peering into the gloomy opening, you can just make out some stairs disappearing down into the darkness.

If you wish to examine the dead body, turn to **146**.

If you wish to explore the secret passage, turn to **11**.

294

As you pull yourself on to the cold iron platform, you see the maze spread out below you like the surface of a massive brain, each chamber a cell populated with perils created by the devilish imagination of Lord Zahda. A criss-cross of interconnecting walkways is suspended above the maze by gigantic chains that vanish into blackness. You hurry along the iron path towards a staircase that descends to an arch beyond the boundary wall of the maze. As you run through it,

XVII.   The body of a dead man is lying in the fireplace; behind
him, a panel is wedged open and you can just make out some
stairs disappearing into the darkness

you can hear an alarm bell echoing in the vastness above: your escape has not gone unnoticed.

A vaulted corridor lies beyond the arch, which leads to a junction with two exits.

> If you wish to take the passage to your right, turn to **92**.
>
> If you wish to take the passage to your left, turn to **20**.
>
> If you have the Magnakai Discipline of Pathsmanship, turn to **330**.

295

The creatures are so engrossed in their discussion that they do not notice you enter the chamber.

> If you have a bow and wish to use it, turn to **276**.
>
> If you wish to attack them with a hand weapon, turn to **31**.

296

Your killing blow severs the Lekhor's head, sending it spinning into the cold black waters below. A wave of shock ripples through its body and suddenly you are falling, its limp torso still gripped between your feet. Seconds later you hit the lake with a loud splash and sink like a stone.

Turn to **158**.

297

The relentless attack begins to take its toll (lose 2 ENDURANCE points). You know that you cannot resist this psychic battering for much longer – you must do something to stop it.

> If you have a Fireseed and wish to throw it at the plinth, turn to **157**.
>
> If you wish to run forward and physically attack the hand, turn to **116**.
>
> If you wish to run between the two green pillars and escape into the passage beyond, turn to **103**.

298

After a few hundred yards, the passage turns abruptly to the right. Glinting in the dim light is a cluster of huge bubbles floating languidly up and down in the passage ahead. A slight breeze lifts them and slowly they bounce towards you.

> If you wish to push your way past them and continue on your way along the passage, turn to **107**.
>
> If you have a sword and wish to strike out at them, turn to **151**.
>
> If you decide to return to the vault and take the right tunnel, turn to **322**.

299

The warrior leaps to safety as you draw your weapon and face the snarling enemy. 'Brave fool!' you hear him cry, his footfalls fading into the tunnel.

Snickering with delight, like cruel and hungry predators that have trapped themselves a feast, the creatures slink forward. Talons spring from the tips of their webbed fingers and their eyes blaze with wild red fire as they get ready to pounce.

Dhax: COMBAT SKILL 27   ENDURANCE 35

With a trap at your back, you cannot evade combat and must fight these creatures to the death.

If you win the fight, turn to **339**.

300

You fight and claw your way up the crowded staircase and run headlong into the prison complex. Chunks of stone and iron drop from the ceiling as wave upon wave of explosions rock the foundations of the fortress. You cross the complex, cutting down anything that impedes your path, and race along the one corridor that has not been blocked by a rockfall or chasm.

You are halfway up a winding staircase, when there is an enormous groan, followed by a cracking of iron. The creatures around you shriek in terror but their voices are lost as the entire stairway collapses and falls, crumbling and roaring, into a hollow, lava-filled chasm five hundred feet below.

Tragically, your life and your quest end here in the ruins of Kazan-Oud.

301

The snake reveals its fangs. Like great curved broadswords glistening with venom, they shine coldly in the light that pours down through the grating high above. You grip your weapon, bracing your back against the wet stone wall and waiting for the right moment to strike. As the monstrous head sways awkwardly from side to side, you catch sight of a small tunnel cut out of the far wall, which was previously hidden from view by the snake and its nest. Your spirits are raised by the possibility of escaping from this nightmare, but first you must fight the hideous creature.

Unless you have the Magnakai Discipline of Curing, double all ENDURANCE points you lose during this combat due to the venomous bite of the monster.

Giant Hactaraton: COMBAT SKILL 22   ENDURANCE 60

After four rounds of combat you can attempt to evade the creature by crawling into the tunnel; turn to **91**.

If you win the combat, turn to **21**.

302

As you draw level with the plinth, the fingers on the hand begin to move. They rise and fall, drumming a slow and clumsy rhythm on the granite surface. The dull thudding causes your head to ache, and the pain increases with every tap of the swollen black fingers.

If you have the Magnakai Discipline of Psi-screen, turn to **179**.

If you do not possess this skill, turn to **53**.

303

The partly submerged pathway takes you to the fissure. Here, the rustle and slither of unseen things echoes from the inky darkness. Suddenly, the shadow of something round and black breaks through the surface of the lake and a hideous gurgling cry splits the night. It flies straight towards you and you quickly take cover inside the narrow fissure.

Turn to **16**.

304

The footsteps halt but a piercing crack, like that of a whip, breaks the silence. You cry out in pained surprise as an angry red weal opens from your temple to your chin (lose 3 ENDURANCE points). You sense his presence but you cannot see the enemy who dealt you this wound.

If you wish to try to defend yourself against your invisible attacker, turn to **257**.

If you choose to run back along the corridor, turn to **64**.

If you decide to risk jumping into the pit, turn to **275**.

305

The designs are woven from pure gold and silver, studded with gems and semi-precious stones. You marvel at the craftsmanship and beauty of these tapestries – they must be worth many thousands of crowns. One gem in particular catches your eye – a large Diamond. Unable to resist the temptation, you prise it from the cloth and drop it into your pocket (mark this as a Special Item on your *Action Chart*), before leaving the hall by the door.

Turn to **256**.

306

Using your discipline, you focus your attention on the strange triangular plaque fixed to the bars and, gradually, its purpose becomes clear. By finding the total number of triangles contained in the design and turning the pointer to the same number on the dial before pulling the lever, you will ensure that the portcullis opens safely.

Turn back to **11** and study the design. When you think you have the answer, turn to the entry that bears the same number.

307

You sense that the ceiling of mist hides a powerful energy field. Touching such a force barrier, especially when immersed in water, could prove fatal.

If you decide to touch the mist in spite of the danger, turn to **60**.

If you decide to dive down and examine the statue, turn to **168**.

308

A few feet along the tunnel, you notice an irregular square in the floor ahead – the tell-tale sign of a trap. It poses no problem to a warrior of your prowess and you clear it with one bound. Further on, you reach a spiral staircase that leads down to a rough-walled cavern. At the bottom of the staircase two tunnels lead away, one to the north and one to the west.

If you wish to enter the north tunnel, turn to **59**.
If you wish to enter the west tunnel, turn to **323**.
If you have the Magnakai Discipline of Nexus, turn to **99**.

309

The descent is slow and arduous. Much of the staircase has been carried away by falling stonework from the battlements, and you have to contend with a rain of molten ash and pumice that is erupting from the core of the keep. You take shelter where you can but you dare not linger too long in any one place for fear of being caught in a fissure or a rock slide.

By the time you reach the beach, your cloak and hood are smouldering and the soles of your boots have nearly melted. Many of the creatures of Kazan-Oud have escaped before you and they crowd the beach, clawing and biting each other in a frenzy of terror. The lake is choked with their dead, and the black sand is barely visible beneath the carpet of carcasses. You fend off the crazed beasts as best you can, but to stay on the beach would be suicidal.

If you choose to climb up the rocks and dive into the lake, turn to **254**.
If you decide to fight your way down to the old stone jetty, turn to **122**.

310

You tie a loop in one end of the rope and scan the

opposite side for a secure target. A spur of stone near the centre of the shattered staircase looks promising, and you aim for that. On your second attempt the rope finds its mark and tightens around the stone. You waste no time crossing the gap, and within minutes, you are safely across and climbing the few remaining stairs to the breached fortress wall.

Turn to **27**.

311

You are quick to regain your balance and press on regardless of your stinging wounds (lose 2 ENDURANCE points). Once more the whip cracks but you are now out of range of its cruel bite.

Turn to **6**.

312

There is a faint click and the panel slides open to reveal a set of steps leading down to a sturdy wooden door, reinforced with bands of studded iron.

If you wish to investigate further, turn to **37**.
If you choose not to enter, turn to **102**.

313

The lack of oxygen is making you light-headed (lose 3 ENDURANCE points), but you try to ignore the pain and continue.

Pick a number from the *Random Number Table*.

If your ENDURANCE points total is 10 or more, turn to **4**.
If it is 9 or less, turn to **263**.

314

Blinking away the tears, you concentrate all of your discipline and skill on finding a target in the billowing smoke. A shadow to your left betrays a creature that is crawling along the walkway on its belly. You lower your bow and fire. An instant later, a howl of rage and pain confirms a hit. The scream quickly fades, as the creature rolls over and falls to its doom.

Suddenly a shape hurtles out of the smoke, clawing and biting savagely at your face and arms. You drop your bow and unsheathe a weapon just in time to receive its attack.

Dhax: COMBAT SKILL 20   ENDURANCE 28

You may evade combat at any time by running into the archway opposite; turn to **277**.
If you win the combat, turn to **141**.

315 – *Illustration XVIII*

The entire corridor shakes with the violence of a series of eruptions that tears rock and iron with ease. All around you Zahda's loathsome minions run in utter panic, their voices rising to a cacophony of terror as frantically they seek to escape from Kazan-Oud.

Jets of flaming gas erupt from splits in the floor as you sprint, crawl, climb and jump over the obstacles hurled in your path by the dying fortress. Creatures from the maze now stalk these levels, adding to the carnage and panic as they consume the unfortunates who cross their path.

You cover a mile of broken passage before you find an undamaged staircase. It winds upwards into the

XVIII.   The entire corridor shakes with the violence of a series of eruptions that tears rock and iron with ease

316

dust-choked darkness, and, as you pound its rubble-strewn steps, your feet are licked by flames. Below, the screams are drowned by the deafening roar of fire and explosion; above, there is nothing but darkness.

You are nearing the point of collapse when suddenly you emerge from the blackness into the glare of daylight. You stagger and fall, momentarily blinded. As your eyes gradually become accustomed to the light, you cast your gaze over the broken battlements of the castle keep and see the glimmering waters of Lake Khor far below.

The walls of the fortress are crumbling rapidly and the ground is alive with constant vibration. You run headlong through the ruined main gate as bolts of lightning are drawn from the sky by the dying power of Kazan-Oud. At the top of a ruined staircase, you stare down at the shore far below.

If you wish to descend the steps to the old stone jetty, turn to **122**.

If you choose to make your way to the beach, turn to **309**.

If you decide to dive from the cliff into the water far below, turn to **254**.

316

You are in combat with four armoured Beastmen. They attack simultaneously and you must fight them as one enemy.

Zahda Beastmen: COMBAT SKILL 30   ENDURANCE 39

If you win the combat in three rounds or less, turn to **248**.

If combat lasts longer than three rounds, turn to **160**.

317

Filling your hand with the hilt of the sun-sword, you unsheathe its golden blade and sever the tendril with one stroke. But instead of blood, or what would pass for blood in the body of this ghastly creature, a flame bursts into life like a spluttering fuse. The brain ceases to move, hovering motionless above the sand, as the spitting flame burns fiercely along its thin tube of sundered flesh.

Turn to **170**.

318

The cloying smell of damp and decay grows steadily stronger, and you are forced to cover your nose with your cloak to block out the sickly stench. The tunnel twists to the right and you notice a small iron door set into the wall ahead, and a narrow staircase descending into the gloom.

If you wish to investigate the door, turn to **262**.
If you decide to descend the stairs, turn to **11**.

319

Taking up a position to one side of the tunnel, you press yourself flat against the wall and wait for the best moment to strike. Four warriors, dark and grim, march into the hall in single file. At first sight you mistake them for Drakkarim, for their black armour and skull-like helmets are identical to those worn by the evil human warriors who serve the Darklords of Helgedad. As you launch your attack, you see their features and realize that they cannot possibly be human. Great sloping shoulders support their unnaturally long arms; yellow-clawed hairy hands grip axes and spears of rough-wrought iron; and behind them swing long, tufted tails, like those of lions.

Your first blow shears through the backplate of the last warrior in the line, causing him to howl like a demon and collapse in a crumpled heap at your feet. The others spin to face you, their reactions battle-swift, their weapons raised to counter your threat. The leader throws open his visor to reveal a boar-like snout and tusks. He bellows a fearsome growl and stabs at you with his spear. The others echo his cry and close around you. You cannot evade combat and must fight all three as one enemy.

Zahda Beastmen: COMBAT SKILL 28   ENDURANCE 35

If you win the combat, turn to **56**.

320

You race back towards the corner but a slab of smooth stone is rumbling into view, sealing off the only exit. You are forced to stop and face the fiery attacker.

Turn to **126**.

321

Nothing seems to happen. The buttons remain depressed and the concealed door remains closed. You are about to step away from the sarcophagus when there is a faint click and the panel slides open. You chance a cautious glance inside and see a set of steps leading down to a stout wooden door, its gnarled timber studded and reinforced with bands of iron.

If you wish to enter the sarcophagus, turn to **37**.
If you choose not to enter, turn to **102**.

322

You walk along the passage for several minutes until it turns sharply to the left. Cautiously you peer around the corner, your basic Kai instincts alerting you to a potential threat. Peering down, you see a beam of light shining from one side of the corridor to the other. The passage ahead looks no different to those in the rest of the maze but you feel sure that it contains a deadly trap.

If you wish to step over the beam of light and continue along the passage, turn to **88**.
If you choose to walk through the beam, turn to **240**.

323

You thread your way through a network of empty passages and chambers. Twice you are forced to hide when groups of black-armoured warriors appear unexpectedly. At first you think that they are Drakkarim, evil humans who serve the Darklords of Helgedad, but their unnaturally long arms and the tails that swing behind them soon dispel that fear, replacing it with a far greater one.

At the bottom of a narrow winding stairway, you arrive at a small but opulently furnished chamber, its walls hung with beautiful tapestries, undamaged by the damp that pervades the upper levels of the fortress. It looks as if you have reached a dead end and you are about to turn back when you notice a small door tucked away in one corner of the room.

If you wish to open the door, turn to **256**.
If you decide to take a closer look at the tapestries, turn to **305**.

324

The heat is unbearable (lose 4 ENDURANCE points). In order to keep your boots from catching fire, and in the hope of reaching a cooler section of the tube, you force yourself to run deeper into the oven-like tunnel.

Turn to **24**.

325

You strike the seething water with a mighty splash and sink like a stone. The sharp tang of the lake fills your mouth and its icy-cold embrace numbs your muscles. Your first impulse on hitting the water is to lash out with your arms and swim, but you are hampered by a mass of plant life that coils around your flailing limbs. Desperate for air, you hack blindly at the weeds that now threaten to drag you to a watery grave.

Fight the combat as normal. However, due to your lack of air, you must automatically deduct 2 ENDURANCE points for every round that you fight.

Black Lakeweed: COMBAT SKILL 10   ENDURANCE 50

If you survive the struggle, turn to **158**.

326

You make it through the gap with less than an inch to spare. With your stomach churning, you drag yourself to your feet and retrace your steps along the murky tunnel. The familiar red glow of the tunnel you passed earlier appears once more in the gloom ahead.

If you now choose to explore this tunnel, turn to **144**.

If you decide to go back to the rough-walled cavern and take the west tunnel instead, turn to **323**.

327

Gulping a lungful of air, you dive below the water and focus your Magnakai Discipline on the lock, willing it to open. It is a severe test of your skill, made all the more difficult by the lack of air.

Pick a number from the *Random Number Table*. If you have reached the rank of Primate, add 2 to the number you have picked.

If your total is 4 or less, turn to **184**.

If it is 5 or more, turn to **4**.

328

The slinking creatures fill the narrow walkway, offering themselves as easy targets to your bow. Pick a number from the *Random Number Table*. If you have the Magnakai Discipline of Weaponskill with bow, add 3 to the number you have picked. If you have completed the Lore-circle of Fire, add 1.

If your total score is now 0–4, turn to **232**.

If it is 5 or more, turn to **67**.

329

You ponder the problem for several minutes, using your natural Kai instincts to the full as you try to discover which of the numbers on the dial will open the portcullis. The image of four numbers – three, nine, thirteen, and thirty-three – fill your mind but, try as you might, you cannot determine which of them is correct.

> If you wish to turn the pointer to number three, before pulling the lever, turn to **3**.
> If you wish to turn the pointer to number nine, turn to **9**.
> If you wish to turn the pointer to number thirteen, turn to **13**.
> If you wish to turn the pointer to number thirty-three, turn to **33**.

330

Your Pathsmanship skill reveals that the passage to your left leads to a complex of prison cells; the passage to your right leads to a guard room and torture chamber.

If you decide to take the left passage, turn to **20**.
If you choose the right passage, turn to **92**.

331

Your death is mercifully swift. As the mouth of the monster closes around your upper body, you are paralysed by corrosive saliva and so spared the agony of being eaten alive.

Your life and your quest end here.

332

You leap forward and strike left and right, ripping through the startled guards and meeting little resistance. Two fall and a third steps forward, his sword yet to clear his scabbard. You hit him below the chin and see his beast-like eyes roll up in sudden agony as blood gushes from under his helmet. As he sinks, gurgling, to his knees, you see the fourth warrior disappearing down the corridor, his cries of alarm reverberating along the passage.

If you wish to run after him, turn to **195**.
If you decide to enter the chamber and attempt to escape along the opposite corridor, turn to **69**.

333

As you place the key into the tiny keyhole, you feel your fingers tingle. There is a soft noise like rushing wind, then, suddenly, the key vanishes from your grip (erase this Special Item from your *Action Chart*). Soundlessly, the great door swings open to reveal a plain stone room. You enter and, as the door closes, you notice a coiled snake etched deep into its surface.

334

Carved in the centre of its scaly coils is the number **123**. Make a note of this number in the margin of your *Action Chart* – it may be of use to you at a later stage of your adventure.

Beside the closed door, hanging in a rack suspended from the ceiling, is a Spear and a Quarterstaff. Both weapons are in remarkably fine condition despite the warm, damp air. At the other side of the room, two torchlit tunnels descend to the north and the east.

If you wish to enter the north tunnel, turn to **187**.
If you wish to enter the east tunnel, turn to **101**.
If you have the Magnakai Discipline of Paths-manship, turn to **139**.

334

'Good!' booms the voice of Zahda as you enter the passage; 'the cowards of Elzian have at last sent a warrior worthy of my maze.'

The words conjure up a picture of Lord Zahda seated on his golden throne, with the object of your quest, the Lorestone of Herdos, suspended above it. The image strengthens your resolve to survive this accursed maze and escape. If you can then find your way back to Zahda's throne-hall, the success of your quest will be within your grasp.

You walk along the passage, your mind filled with the possible problems and perils you might have to over-come. One such problem looms into view as the passage takes a sharp turn.

Turn to **100**.

335

A rickety, hunch-backed creature, swathed in a hooded robe, approaches the platform on which you stand manacled to the wall. With an efficiency born of practice, quickly he strips you of all your weapons and hands them to an ugly-faced dwarf, hovering at his side. The dwarf looks at the Sommerswerd with an appraising eye, then raises it above his head to show it to his master. Before he can speak, there is a sudden roar, as a bolt of golden energy engulfs the hilt. Screaming with pain, the dwarf drops the sword and cradles his smoking hand, his fingers now missing half their length. You are unable to hide your smile and are quickly punished for your insolence. The robed creature strikes you across the face, gashing your cheek with its rough, warty fist (lose 1 ENDURANCE point).

'Take him to the maze,' commands white-haired Lord Zahda, 'and leave the sword for me.'

The Sommerswerd rises into the air and floats towards the golden throne on a cushion of blue mist. As you are dragged from the hall in chains, you are taunted by Zahda's cruel laugh and the fear that your quest is now doomed to failure.

Erase all weapons and weapon-like Special Items from your *Action Chart* and make a note of them on a separate piece of paper in case you should rediscover them at a later stage of your adventure.

Now turn to **286**.

336

A new sound is added to the terrible squeals of the hungry rats: the sound of splintering wood. In less than a minute, your small boat is completely devoured, leaving no trace of its ever having existed. The jagged rocks cut into your hands and knees but you are oblivious to the pain as you clamber across them to the beach beyond. You set off at a run, but the fine, black sand closes around your ankles, and your legs ache violently with every desperate step.

A glance over your shoulder warns you that the pack are gaining ground rapidly; they will be on you before you reach the rocky base of Kazan-Oud. Then suddenly the squealing stops; the black tide has halted at the edge of the beach. Their white teeth snap on empty air and hungry eyes watch your every movement, but every single one of them is rooted to the rocks.

As you turn to make your escape, you wonder why the rats no longer pursue you. Less than ten feet ahead lies the horrific answer to your question.

Turn to **221**.

337

The wall is descending fast; there is very little space left through which to escape.

Pick a number from the *Random Number Table*. If you have the Magnakai Discipline of Huntmastery, you may add 3 to the number you have picked.

If your total is now *0–4*, turn to **237**.
If it is 5 or more, turn to **188**.

338

Your Magnakai Discipline, heightened by the discovery of the Lorestone of Herdos, screams a warning that the stairs to the cell complex are doomed to disaster. Your senses tell you that by staying on this level and following the corridor to the far side of the subterranean lair, you will be sure of finding a safe route up to the surface.

Turn to **315**.

339

Wisps of smoke are beginning to rise from the dead bodies; suddenly one bursts into flames. Quickly you leap across the slab, away from the heat and choking black fumes, as the others are swallowed by a fire that crackles and spits like an angry demon.

Further along the tunnel, you see the warrior. He is crouching on his heels, his hands resting on the hilt of his sword. A smile spreads across his unshaven face as he sees your approach. 'You're brave, I'll grant you that. There's none I know who'd stand against three hungry Dhax.' He jumps to his feet, sheathes his sword and offers his hand in friendship.

Turn to **12**.

You tell him of your quest and the help the Elder Magi have given to enable you to enter Kazan-Oud. When you recount your air voyage to Herdos aboard Lord Paido's skyship, you notice a tear trickle from the blind man's eye. 'My name is Kasin,' he says, sorrowfully. 'Lord Paido is my brother.'

Pity fills your heart for this unfortunate warrior, for you know that he is doomed to die. Blindness occurs in the final stage of takadea, the disease that is ravaging his body. 'I am beyond help,' he says, his face lined with pain, 'but I can and will help your quest, Kai Lord. Listen to me carefully. There are stairs at the end of the corridor that lead down to the throne-hall of Zahda. At the entrance to the hall there is a tapestry behind which there is a secret passage. It leads to Zahda's throne. Above the throne is the Lorestone you seek, but beware. Zahda has coupled its power to a Doomstone from the realm of Naaros – Zahda draws all his power from this accursed gem. If you are to succeed, you must first destroy the gem or you will surely perish. Sadly I cannot help you escape from Kazan-Oud, for I myself was captured long before I reached the surface, but if you reach the beach, make your way to the old stone jetty. Beneath the steps is the place where I hid my boat.'

He grips your hand in friendship, his face now calm and peaceful. 'When you return to Elzian, tell my brother that my death was not in vain. May the gods protect you, Lone Wolf.'

The sound of approaching guards forces you to leave the cell. As you close the door, you promise that his bravery will live forever in the legends of the Vakeros – his warrior kin.

Turn to **142**.

341

The blood of the dead wolf stains you from head to foot, filling your nose with an acrid smell. With sword in hand, you stare down at the carcass and shiver at the thought of how close you came to death. The dim light grows brighter and for a moment you hear laughter, cold and distant, before the light fades to its usual murky glow and you are surrounded by silence.

Turn to **298**.

342 – *Illustration XIX (overleaf)*

The sphere halts in mid-air less than ten feet from where you stand. It looks like a huge, black human brain studded with large, hairy warts. A whistle, soft but chilling, gradually rises in pitch until it fills your head with agonizing pain. Your fingers tremble and, as your weapon slips from your grasp, a slit opens in the side of the brain. It is a mouth, broad and puffy, with an upper lip that hangs over the lower jaw like milk boiling over the pan. A long tendril of flesh emerges from the mouth and snakes through the air towards your throat.

If you possess the Magnakai Discipline of Psi-screen, turn to **217**.

If you possess the Magnakai Discipline of Animal Control, turn to **35**.

If you possess neither of these skills, turn to **143**.

XIX. The sphere halts in mid-air: it looks like a huge, black human brain studded with large, hairy warts

343

The chamber is well lit by a row of torches lining all four walls, and there is very little furniture to hide behind.

Pick a number from the *Random Number Table*. If you have the Magnakai Discipline of Invisibility add 3 to the number you have picked.

If your total is now 7 or less, turn to **69**.
If it is *8* or more, turn to **197**.

344

Your hand strikes something invisible set close to the edge of the pit – the beginning of a magically hidden bridge. Your fingers tell you that it is a plank, for it feels very thin and narrow. Suddenly the footsteps halt. There is a piercing crack, like that of a whip, and an angry red weal opens across the back of your hand (lose 2 ENDURANCE points). You sense his presence but you cannot see the enemy who dealt you this wound.

If you wish to step on to the invisible bridge, turn to **166**.
If you wish to try to fight your unseen enemy, turn to **257**.

345

The warrior makes no attempt to parry your attack, and your blow rips deeply into his unguarded chest. He stares at you in disbelief as he clutches at his wound and drops heavily to his knees. 'Why?' he croaks, as his eyelids flicker and close.

346

A howl of maniacal glee arises from the black creatures. As the warrior falls into the smoky abyss, they slink towards you with long, loping strides.

If you wish to stand and fight these creatures, turn to **249**.

If you decide to evade them by escaping into the archway opposite, turn to **241**.

346

Desperately you tap the wall with the hilt of your weapon, praying for the dull, tell-tale thud of a thin or hollow partition through which you might effect an escape. The walls yield no such sound but in the roof you discover an old trap-door hatch sealed off with bricks and mortar. The faint glimmer of light seeping through a hairline crack fills you with renewed hope.

With a flurry of blows the mortar crumbles and the bricks split and fall. Without waiting for the dust to settle, you climb through the jagged hole and emerge into a hall that is filled with a damp and earthy smell. Two rows of great stone pillars support the roof and a huge, granite sarcophagus stands in the centre of the floor. From within a black tunnel to your right, you hear the clanking of armour and the sound of approaching footsteps.

If you wish to hide behind one of the pillars, turn to **110**.

If you wish to leave the hall by a tunnel to your left, turn to **201**.

If you wish to lie in ambush for whatever is approaching the hall, turn to **319**.

347

You snatch the whistle to your lips and blow. Instantly, the slimy creature rears up, its short rubbery legs scrabbling the air in agony as the ultra high-pitched sound destroys its sensitive nervous system.

As it twists back on itself, its head disappears into the misty ceiling. There is an ear-splitting crack and blue lightning engulfs the creature, crackling snake-like around its neck, and filling the corridor with the stench of burning meat. The creature thrashes wildly for several minutes, and when its gruesome dance finally ends the canopy of mist is no longer there. In the darkness above, you see a walkway and an observation platform.

If you wish to climb the body of the dead worm and pull yourself on to the platform, turn to **294**.

If you prefer to climb over the carcass and continue along the corridor, turn to **46**.

348

Shortly you arrive at another stone staircase. This one is intact, however, and ascends to a cave-like entrance in the sheer rock wall. You cannot follow the beach any further, for a salient of the wall blocks your way. Moreover, the weather is getting worse with every passing minute and you need to seek shelter from the coming storm.

By the time you have climbed all the way to the cave, the storm has broken. As you stand in the entrance, the rain-filled wind lashes you mercilessly and the ground shudders with every clap of thunder. The faint green glow of the power-shield is the only source of light and you enter cautiously. You are soon swallowed up by darkness and your progress becomes painfully slow.

> If you have a Kalte Firesphere, a Lantern or a Torch and Tinderbox, turn to **49**.
> If you have none of these Items, turn to **277**.

349

As soon as you step into the ruby corridor the horse-shoe arch turns completely opaque. You try to go back but the milky-white barrier will not let you pass. Soon, the skull appears once more, but this time its message chills you to the core:

'The path you have chosen leads to the heart of the maze,
And there you are doomed to eke out your days.'

It is a prophecy that will be fulfilled. You have ventured too deep into Zahda's maze and the exits are now closed off forever. It may interest you to learn that you survived at the core of the maze for three weeks, a feat that earned you the respect of Lord Zahda, but one that did not persuade him to spare you your life.

Your life and your quest end here.

350 – *Illustration XX (overleaf)* >

As soon as you have passed through the power-shield, you are greeted like a hero by a huge flotilla of fishing vessels and trading barges. An hour ago, upon seeing the eruption of Kazan-Oud, every boat in Herdos set sail for the shield, for the eruption signalled the end of the bane that had haunted Dessi for hundreds of years. Now they cheer the Sommlending warrior who has delivered them from Dessi's evil shadow. Eager hands pull you aboard Lord Ardan's caravel and a fanfare salute is sounded by the trumpeteers of his Vakeros guards.

'We are forever in your debt, Lone Wolf,' says Lord Ardan, as he shakes your hand warmly in gratitude and friendship. 'You have achieved what we feared to be impossible and you live to tell the tale. Your bravery is an inspiration to us all.' His words are reinforced by the delirious cheers of his people. He asks of your own quest, and, when you remove the Lorestone of Herdos from the pocket of your tattered and scorched tunic, his eyes widen with amazement.

He bows his head and says in a solemn and respectful voice, 'My lord, you stand upon the threshold of greatness. Your purpose and your destiny are known to the Elder Magi, for we have awaited your coming for many thousands of years. Our survival and the survival of all we cherish rests on the success of your Magnakai quest. The time has come, Lone Wolf, for you to learn our wisdom, for we are of the same blood, you and I, and our fate is bound together. We

XX.   'We are forever in your debt, Lone Wolf,' says Lord Ardan,
as he shakes your hand warmly

will prepare you for your next quest, for the Lorestone you must find next exists in the land that was once our home, in the temple that was once our most sacred place of worship, in the chamber where our master first appeared to us.'

Your quest has succeeded, for the strength and wisdom of the Lorestone of Herdos is now a part of your body and spirit. But there is much for you to learn from the Elder Magi as they prepare you for the most challenging of the Magnakai quests you have yet to attempt, a quest that will take you deep into the hostile swamps of the Danarg, where the evil creatures of Agarash the Damned still thrive and dominate the land.

If you have the courage of a true Kai Master, the secrets of the Elder Magi and the perils of the Danarg await you in Book 8 of the Lone Wolf series entitled:

The Jungle of Horrors

RANDOM NUMBER TABLE

4	6	5	2	8	6	4	0	7	2
5	3	9	8	8	0	4	7	7	5
2	0	5	6	6	9	6	3	6	7
2	2	4	8	8	6	6	9	8	2
4	5	9	0	7	4	8	4	4	0
4	8	2	2	8	7	3	9	5	2
9	4	5	7	7	1	3	8	2	0
6	9	3	5	6	1	8	4	3	0
3	9	6	6	6	1	8	8	1	2
8	6	4	6	0	5	5	0	1	8